Tragedy at Bawley Bay

Elizabeth M Cox

First published in Great Britain in 2017 by
Snow Moon Publications

Printed by Createspace

ISBN 978-1-544-06744-5

Acknowledgements

I would like to thank the Bardstown Writers' Group in Stratford upon Avon whose positive response to my short stories helped me to begin writing again following the deaths of my parents. Thanks also to readers of an early version of this novella for your honest reactions and helpful comments, and to Angela for moral support and encouragement over many years. The expertise and guidance provided by The Hilary Johnson Authors' Advisory Service has also been invaluable.

Tragedy at Bawley Bay is for my mother and everyone
affected by Alzheimer's Disease

One need not be a Chamber – to be Haunted –
One need not be a House –
The Brain has Corridors – surpassing
Material Place –

Emily Dickinson, 'One need not be a Chamber
– to be Haunted', 1862

Contents

Prologue

Dr Westcott's Study, Stone House, Christmas Eve 1928

"Yes, come Gentlemen, sit and thaw yourselves by the fire. Neither of you can leave tonight in this blizzard. The snow is settling fast, and to set off now from this remote spot would be to risk your lives."

As he finished speaking the wind moaned and thrashed a blast of snow against the large bay window, as if to corroborate his warning.

"Thank you, Dr Westcott. It is most good of you," replied Dr Freeman, the younger of the two guests, glancing nervously in the direction of the startling sound.

Dr Westcott also flinched and, endeavouring to compose himself, continued,

"That is quite alright. I am sure you will be able to depart at first light. Otherwise, never fear, my wife will do us chaps proud on the culinary front. Females are so good at arranging the domestic side of things. I would not tell *her* that, of course. Anyway, I have no doubt you will enjoy Christmas Day hospitality here at Stone House and I am sure that whatever preparations you have for the day can be delayed by a few… well… a few hours or so."

Dr Freeman remained silent and stared at his own distorted reflection in the glass. He appeared blurry and dull, he thought, and this tallied with how he felt, although he doubted that the other two would notice. His haziness arose from the wine he had uncharacteristically over-indulged in at dinner, and his mood lowered as he visualised the expressions of disappointment on his daughters' faces when Nurse told them that Mother and Father would not be at home to share the delight of Christmas Day morning.

His meditations were interrupted by Dr Westcott's raised voice,

"Indeed, your being detained overnight is fortuitous, as I urgently need to consult you on a professional concern. I have brought you into my study, so that we can confer in private. I have a strange tale to tell and I had been impatient to relate it to you yesterday evening, but recording the outcome of our latest research was the priority, and that took far longer than I anticipated. I realise that I would have squandered my opportunity to canvass your opinions if this atrocious weather had not arrived.

"Bennett! Offer brandy to our guests. We will be in here for some time, and I fear we may need the courage that such a spirit can bring."

Bennett materialised from the darkness of the doorway,

"Yes, Dr Westcott, right away Sir."

His words were barely audible above the sudden howling of the wind.

"None for me, thank you, Dr Westcott, I have had quite enough al–" commenced Dr Freeman.

"Nonsense, Man. Oh, and I shall need more lamps, Bennett – it is uncommonly gloomy in here."

"Yes Sir."

When Bennett had withdrawn to fulfil his instructions, Dr Westcott continued more quietly,

"Now, where was I? Oh, yes – now that the ladies have retired, I need to inform you both of my discovery – a most disturbing revelation. As you know, I am in the process of verifying the final proofs of our treatise on notable theories pertaining to the peculiar psychiatric characteristics of the female murderer, arising from the examination of prominent asylum cases between 1865 and 1925.

"Incidentally, I have altered the title of the volume to *A History of Insanity Among Female Murderers*. Far more satisfactory and to the point.

"You will not believe it – *I* cannot credit it – but, the day before your arrival yesterday, some papers were unearthed from behind the wooden panelling in the drawing-room – my men stumbled across them during some urgent renovation work and brought them directly to me. They comprise a manuscript plus two brief letters, each written in 1866, as well as a newspaper article dated the previous year.

"Suffice to say, I have examined these documents and decided that they must be destroyed. I will read them to you as a matter of courtesy and, that done, I fully intend to burn them."

"What? What *are* you talking about?" challenged the second listener, Dr Grand.

"As I have said, they *must* be obliterated," retorted Dr Westcott. "I have concluded that should anyone believe them, they would not only throw our findings into doubt but, more seriously for me and mine, threaten the heretofore stainless reputation of my dear departed father."

His face took on a distant expression while he pondered, "By the way, I think it highly unlikely that anyone would accept them as true, but even so... Then again, people can be so easily misled. Anyway, I am certain that you will concur when you have heard what they contain."

"Well, I do not know, destroying official evidence is a potentially serious–" interjected Dr Freeman anxiously.

"As I say, I am sure that you will come around to my way of thinking," insisted Dr Westcott in a threatening tone.

"But what *are* they? *How* do they undermine our work?" demanded Dr Grand.

"Well, if you let me explain, Dr Grand and please keep your voice down," growled Dr Westcott.

"As you know, this residence was formerly The City of London Lunatic Asylum. The manuscript and one of the short letters were written by a personage who was placed under restraint here in 1866, a young murderer named Miss Jane Waterford.

"It is most infuriating, but we have used this d___ lunatic as one of our most significant case histories and referred to her throughout. As I said, I think it most improbable, but if anyone were to accept her story, then they would be forced to deduce that she was neither a killer, nor insane. Do you not see? These letters potentially call into dispute the theories that we have derived from an examination of her case. Think how our standing would be damaged if we published our treatise and this... this fabrication was subsequently broadcast to a gullible public."

"Heavens above! But how on earth does your father's eminence come into question? That is preposterous! Surely?" roared Dr Grand.

"Please do not bellow, Grand!" Dr Westcott boomed back.

"My father was the asylum superintendent at the time of her committal. It seems that, despite being the recipient of these papers subsequent to Miss Waterford being placed under his charge, he failed to instigate an investigation that might have led to her incarceration order being quashed. The drawing-room used to function as the superintendent's office, and I can only assume that he was responsible for hiding them. There is even a suggestion of bribery!"

"Good Lord! So, what exactly does the correspondence consist of?" probed Dr Freeman.

"The manuscript – a protracted declaration of innocence addressed to my father – is dated Christmas Day 1866 and recounts the events that led to Miss Waterford being locked away that same day. Obviously, they are told from her perspective. But, as I have already said, if the account is true then she was neither guilty nor mad. The plea remains unsigned, but is written in an identical hand to one of the shorter letters – a copy of the original – penned on December 22nd that same year, which *is* signed by Miss Waterford. Undoubtedly, she composed them before she was brought here, but I could find no reference to them in her medical record. Oh, and there is a brief addendum to the manuscript introduced by her two days after her confinement. The third letter is a reply to her correspondence and was written by her addressee on the following day – December 23rd, I mean. As I mentioned, I also came across this newspaper article from the G____ Reporter secreted between the manuscript pages which, as you will hear, is closely associated with the other items."

Dr Westcott held up the yellowing paper in such a way that his colleagues could make out the headline, "Tragic Accident at Bawley Bay: Fifty Year Anniversary."

"How astonishing!" exclaimed Dr Freeman. "Do you know anything about the woman? I do not recall being involved in reviewing her case history," he continued, trying not to show that he was feeling uplifted by this intriguing turn of events which, if true, might burst Dr Westcott's pomposity somewhat.

"Yes, a few details," replied Dr Westcott, eyeing him closely.

"Evidently Miss Waterford had been residing in G____ which, at that time, was a fashionable resort on the River Thames. She was a lonely spinster who sought solace in teaching the children of the destitute at the Ragged School. She was placed in the asylum on Christmas Day 1866 having been accused by a respectable gentleman of the premeditated murder of two women, as well as attempting to take his life without provocation. The case was never presented for public trial and so her guilt remained unproven, but she was certified as insane and detained here instead."

"Yes, yes, we know all about that. I recollect that she was released after a couple of years. So, no harm done," blustered Dr Grand.

"Not so, Grand!" Dr Westcott thundered, despite his own admonitions to speak in hushed tones.

"You must be confusing her with another of our female lunatics. According to Mrs Baker, my housekeeper, Miss Waterford tried to escape from the asylum on numerous occasions. Mrs Baker's late mother worked here as Matron of the female side and remembered Miss Waterford clearly. When Mrs Baker was a young girl, her mother used to enthral her with gossip about all the patients' antics. Yes, Miss Waterford was unsuccessful in her attempts to run away and was repeatedly brought back. Of course, such imprudent conduct took a toll on her health and she died – well yes, let us just say she died – a year or so after her incarceration. Her medical records confirm this, at least."

"That is so often the case," said Dr Freeman sadly, but immediately brightened up,

"What did the physicians diagnose her with? Do you think they accepted bribes as well?"

"Impossible to say for certain because the records appear credible. Of course, back then, some sixty years ago, they lacked the advances in medical psychiatry that we have today, as well as our consequent insights into the myriad nervous disorders that are peculiarly female in nature.

"Despite these difficulties, both physicians diagnosed her with monomania, justifying it on the basis that they perceived her version of events to be utterly absurd. As you know, monomania, or partial insanity, is where – well, let me refresh your memories and read you James Cowles Prichard's 1835 definition in *A Treatise on Insanity and Other Disorders Affecting the Mind* – monomania is where,

> the understanding is partially disordered, or under the influence of some particular illusion, referring to one subject, and involving one train of ideas, while the intellectual powers appear, when exercised on other subjects, to be in a great measure unimpaired.

"Thus, the sufferer has an obsessional focus on a single fancy, always a misconception, from which they cannot be distracted or convinced of its lack of veracity.

"Oh, and one physician, a Dr Reed, pronounced a secondary diagnosis. His deliberations show that he considered moral insanity due to her unnatural inclinations and deviant behaviour."

"Of what nature might those have been?" enquired Dr Grand.

"For Heaven's sake Man, that will become clear when I read the documents to you. Where was I? Yes, this notion was rejected as it would have amounted to an admission that her explanation was true, because moral insanity has no associated loss of reasoning capabilities, nor is the patient subject to hallucinations. Clearly, that would not have served the purpose.

"No, he decreed that her mind was deranged, and substantiated this by demonstrating that she was unable to distinguish between the substance of her dreams and actuality. Crucially, linked to this, he also found that she failed to distinguish between the real world and the fabricated realms conjured up by her excessive devouring of novels.

"Miss Waterford played into her accuser's hands nicely on this point, because her statement shows her to have been a voracious consumer of the most unsuitable material – yes indeed, most perilous for a girl – reading matter of a sensational and morbid character. As we know, ingesting such novels causes the over-excitement... indeed, the unbalancing of girls' delicate nervous systems. Without doubt, the female type lacks the male's cerebral and rationalising faculties, but has a more impressionable nature and so absorbing sensationalist fiction in particular, causes the over-stimulation of her emotions, leading to hysteria and other nervous diseases. Naturally, as a malleable girl, Miss Waterford would have identified with a duplicitous, violent and ultimately insane character such as Lady Audley. Yes... yes... I am afraid the outcome was a foregone conclusion."

"Well, that seems a terribly outdated view in this day and age, Dr Westcott," suggested Dr Freeman tentatively.

"In addition, *if* I may continue Dr Freeman, Miss Waterford grew up lacking maternal counsel in the matter of compulsory reading, advice manuals and the like, vital in preparing her for sacred self-sacrificing duties as dependant wife and mother. With such guidance she could have become one of the moral guardians of the future leaders of our nation. Whereas, instead, her failure to marry meant that she had far too much idle time on her hands, which she spent in the recreational digesting of these unhealthy novels. The chronicle of corruption and unrepressed agitation told in this manuscript is the inevitable fateful result. It is a baneful warning to all fathers and husbands.

"I do not allow my angels – my wife and daughters – to see anything that I have not sanctioned, you know – even now."

"Really," muttered Dr Freeman, under his breath.

"Quite so. Quite so. Well, that all seems perfectly reasonable to me," concluded Dr Grand dismissively. "I do not think that we have anything to worry about, nor do I believe you need to be concerned for your father's name."

"Yes, so I believed," Dr Westcott became animated again, "until I read these documents! You must hear me out Gentlemen. We must take them seriously. What if there is some truth in them? We must consider the implications."

Dr Grand and Dr Freeman looked askance at Dr Westcott. His overwrought manner was most out of character.

Dr Westcott took a deep breath and resumed,

"However, before I continue, I assume that I have your assurance that you will not discuss any of this with another soul, and especially not with the ladies. As you will hear, Sapphism is involved (or Romantic Friendship as it would have been termed back then); an astonishing coincidence given the recent prosecution and banning of Hall's *The Well of Loneliness* for obscenity. Quite the right verdict, as I am sure you will agree. We do not want our wives and daughters reading that sort of dangerous nonsense."

"Well, I–" began Dr Freeman.

Once again, Dr Westcott persisted without waiting for his colleague to continue,

"As I was saying, the ladies must not be subjected to any aspect of this state of affairs and so Bennett will stand guard at the door. This will allow me to relate the entire narrative from beginning to end without interruption."

"Yes, well, let's make a start, shall we?" urged Dr Grand impatiently.

However, they suffered a further hiatus while they awaited Bennett's return.

Aftermath

Miss Jane Waterford, at Home, Christmas Day Morning 1866 (Tuesday)

They will come for me later today – those wretched souls from the lunatic asylum. I must get away before they arrive. But no, I am certain he will have sent someone to watch the house. Besides, I have nowhere else to go; no one to go to. I doubt Edward will be willing to bear the sight of me now. In any case, strange to say, I feel little more than a dull sense of dread at the prospect of being incarcerated in such a place.

I am told these modern asylums are an improvement on the madhouses – much less brutal since they ceased restraining their charges with vicious contraptions. Although I am certain that wicked man will coerce them into making an exception for me. Yes, they will silence me with a scold's bridle. They say that, in asylums, women live as they would at home, shut indoors and driven insane by interminable domestic duties and needlework. As if that is all women are born to accomplish! At least I shall be residing with other ladies. Perhaps there will be a library…

But I have heard *terrible* stories about them too – I suppose it depends on why they have sent you there. Kathryn told me tales of atrocious deeds – butchery I mean – being performed on women like us, innocent and sane women at that – to cure them of unladylike behaviour, she said. I will just have to take my chances.

Yet (and this seems bizarre, even to me) there is actually *attraction* for me, in that place of relative safety, that sanctuary. I feel the need for such protection desperately as I am suffering from a far more acute fear that is raw and chilling, due to another, entirely different reason. Can anything keep me out of harm's way? Sadly, I doubt it – although it horrifies me to think so.

This morning I awoke to the terrifying sound of a woman screaming. At first I thought the cries were Kathryn's, but slowly, and oh so painfully, I realised that they were my own. I did not know what time it was, although I was aware that it was not yet dawn, as all seemed lustreless, silent and still, both within my room and without. I had let the fire die down as I had been desperate to stay awake, and yet I must have slept because I suffered that ghastly nightmare again.

It is always the same gruesome sequence of events: I am Lizzie Hexam, Gaffer Hexam's loving daughter but grudging helper, just like the opening scene of Mr Dickens' latest story, *Our Mutual Friend*. Kathryn and I had been reading the instalments together, before... Kathryn had every one, all nineteen stacked neatly on the table in the corner of her room. I do not think she would have persevered with them if I had not badgered her. But I did not know then... I just... I did not know. I am holding the rowing boat steady while my father conducts his grisly business of recovering and robbing corpses from the filthy, rushing waters of the River Thames at London. But then, suddenly, unlike Mr Dickens' account, just as it is being hauled onto our vile boat, one grotesque, pale and bloated cadaver opens its eyes inhumanly wide and throws its arms around my neck in a final, desperate clutch at life. I can even smell her putrid flesh – for I know it is a woman – in my lurid dream. No matter how hard I struggle I cannot extricate myself from its vice-like grip or turn away from the intensity of the opaque and lifeless stare emanating from remorseful, half-closed eyes. Immediately, the weight of it starts to drag me down towards the icy brown water.

As I say, this morning, just as I was about to plunge into the freezing depths, I awoke screaming in the way I had witnessed Kathryn awake on so many occasions. During our time together I had been at a loss to comprehend her obsessive fear of drowning in the murky waters of the Thames. Of course, there are abundant drownings as well as narrow escapes in *Our Mutual Friend* and, as we came across each one, I had not understood her morbid fascination nor the extent of her terror. Indeed, in the end, I had become somewhat irritated by her fixation. Tragically, everything has become all too clear to me over recent days. But now, of course, it is too late.

My dread of this recurring nightmare has meant that for the last few nights I have felt it safer to sleep for as short a time as possible, and preferably not at all. As a consequence, I feel light-headed, dizzy even, and tearful; but not simply for that reason alone. It is a terrible thing when being conscious brings no comfort, nor offers respite from the horrors of the world of nightmares. The haunting of my waking hours has been worse – much, much worse. These – what should I call them? – appalling, yes, appalling – happenings have left my nerves frayed and my mind utterly disturbed. I am becoming fearful myself, that I really am becoming insane. Yet these frightful events, which are as inexplicable to me now as they were then, did occur; I knew deep down, even then, that I had not invented them.

Nevertheless, that malicious being has convinced the authorities that I have lost my mind, and that I should be restrained in that great isolated mausoleum, the City of London Lunatic Asylum. They are going to shut me away, just like they did Lady Audley. Indeed, because of his devious actions (he wants me to be put away before the Police uncover too much through their investigations, you see), I have been visited by two physicians in the middle of the night, one following the other, asking question after question. They have both signed the necessary medical certificates. That is all he needs to obtain the order. Signed them on my behalf too, as if what I think does not matter! I know he has put them up to it. He will have bribed them to do it, like that heinous Count Fosco. They did not even tell me what they were writing about me – my supposed diagnosis, I mean. And, as an additional insult, they are sending me to a pauper asylum, as if I have no money to my name! As far as I am concerned, *he* should be incarcerated, and in prison too, but they were only too willing to believe *his* version of events rather than mine. He has convinced them all that I am a madwoman, a danger to others (by which he means himself, of course). Obviously, as a woman I have no power to resist. What authority does any woman have, let alone one regarded as insane?

I would wager he will not go to the Police to press charges about the incident in the cemetery, though – I am quite sure he does not want them raking over those awful events of 1815. In any case, I acted in self-defence. I did what anyone would have done...

They are not interested in anything George has to say either... I mean... about what happened on the steamboat ferry. Worse still, my father's dear friend, the one person who might have saved me, failed to arrive home last night as expected. That sinister creature tells me he is dead and I have no reason to disbelieve him. Nor do I expect there were any other witnesses, up on the deck of the steamer. It was cold, so cold... everyone was down below in the warmth of the saloon.

***

Such are my thoughts in my last precious hours at home and my mood is as bleak as my dark and bitterly cold room. As I struggle to sit up in bed, it is only when I hear drops of water drip like rain upon my bedclothes, that I realise I am the cause of them. Funnels of salty water are overflowing my eyes and streaming down my cheeks and neck. My body might still be at liberty, but my brain is already shackled in heavy chains. How will I survive such ravaging feelings of grief that grip my heart like the talons of an eagle pinioning its helpless prey? I have no answers.

My mind performs cruel tricks on me, forcing me to play a sinister game of forgetting and remembering. I feel constantly on edge and my thoughts flit inconsolably from one state to the other. I forget, momentarily, that Kathryn is gone and then, without warning, the memory and the horror of it all break into my consciousness, bringing a further stabbing pain and yet another smothering layer of grief and dark despair.

I would give anything not to have to face this day. I yearn to remain burrowed within the sheets and blankets, like the velveteen mole that stays underground in safe, earthy passages, undisturbed by turbulent storms above.

Despite my apprehension of what lies ahead, I climb wearily from my bed and light a candle from the dying embers of the fire with a shaking hand. My body feels heavy with fatigue as I stand and peer through the bedroom windowpane which, although clouded by condensed water and the intricate patterns of a thick layer of ice, allows me to gain a partial view of Crooked Lane. Although deserted now, I envisage it will soon be thronging with tradesmen and women from the outlying farms, bringing their produce to market.

It strikes me as strange that other people's lives will be carrying on in their customary, everyday routines, whereas mine is about to undergo such an abrupt and seemingly irreversible transformation. Indeed, it is my usual custom to purchase provisions at the market, but there is no point today as, by tomorrow, I will be gone. But no, I am disoriented, it is Christmas Day – today the streets will remain as empty as I feel inside. How much more desolate to think of spending this day, of all days, completely alone and waiting. Perhaps they will not come for me on this most Holy of days, after all.

Looking beyond the lane I catch a glimpse of the Thames despite the gloomy sky. Menacing clouds obscure the moon and both the heavens and the water seem to mirror each other, appearing blacker still. I can hardly bear to contemplate the deceitful river, which I had thought Kathryn and I both loved so well. Our river, we had fondly named it, although now I wonder whether, by this, we had both meant different things. It seems astonishing how little we understand what is occurring in other people's minds – even those we love – especially when they prevent us from knowing what they are thinking or seeing who they really are. I feel bewildered as I can no longer rely upon any of my former perceptions of the person I loved with all my heart.

Unexpectedly, the clouds part to reveal a moon whose intense light turns the river into a mass of dancing silver. It is a strange, eerie half-light – a most unsettling colourless borderland, seemingly neither day nor night. Suddenly I see her. She appears to be standing on the bank of the river, staring directly at me. She is beckoning me to her. Her face is pale and wears a heart-rending, imploring expression of – what is it – anxiety, fear, maybe even terror? I hear a voice, her voice, reverberate around the lane. I catch her words,

"I love you. Come! Come!"

"So she does love me! Perhaps she *had* been trying to save me from harm," I exclaim to the empty room.

My heart is pounding and I feel as though I am suffocating. I wrestle with the part of myself that just wants to rush to her and hold her in my arms. I claw at the wintry glass separating me from her and cry out like an animal in pain,

"Oh Kathryn, no, please no, it cannot be."

Even after the devastating events of yesterday, it is still not over, nor ever will it be. How am I to bear it? I turn away and, when I summon the courage to steal a second look, she has gone.

My mind is in such a state of confusion that I am left unsure whether I have imagined her. I do not know what to think anymore as all my certainties about the separation between life and death have been overturned during the previous few days. Then harsh reality hits me, like the kick of a mule, as I know she *could not* have really been there, watching me in that way. She has gone from me forever. I crumple into my beloved mother's rocking chair weeping convulsively, while it moves rhythmically of its own accord as if trying to console me. My crying gradually ceases, like the inevitable winding down of a clockwork toy, and I comfort myself with the recollection that I have not always been of this miserable and terror-stricken disposition. In fact, the last year has been the happiest of my life; that is, until *she* – Eleanor – came between us.

But wait, I am getting ahead of myself. I must begin my letter to Dr Westcott, the asylum superintendent, appealing to him to revoke my incarceration order. I fear he is dishonest and in league with my tormentor, but it is my only hope. Hope is all that remains for me. They… they must… they must protect me from Eleanor too. Yes, I need to write everything down from the beginning…

I fumble for my pen, ink and paper and, with a hand that trembles from both the cold and raw fear, begin to write my ghastly tale. At once there comes a loud rapping on the front door of the house. Already in a state of great agitation, the sudden noise so shocks my senses that my heart seems to stop. I dress hastily and stumble to the door with the full expectation that I will be greeted by the sight of the loathsome asylum creatures. That they have come for me before I have been able to record my side of the story, as calmly and logically as I can manage, seems unjust. Shall I open the door? If it is them, it is unlikely that they will leave until they have achieved their mission. As I open it I am met, not by the officers from the asylum, but by George, my ally and good friend. He looks exhausted and haggard, with dark rings encircling his eyes. I stand aside so that he can enter the house, but he refrains from doing so, removing his cap whilst saying diplomatically,

"I won't come in Miss, as I can see you're not ready for visitors, but I thought you ought to know that I've searched all night and I haven't found Mrs

Ashburton's body. I've combed the shore both here and over on the Essex side. I've had men out in rowing boats even in the dark of night, but found nothing floating. She wasn't on the ferry when it arrived in London, neither.

"But then, we didn't expect to find her really, did we?"

I am horrified by his words. Everything seems more upsetting in the harsh light of day. My dread is intensified as I feel that by examining George, I am studying a mirror; the alarm in my own face reflected in his. The fact that George is not a man to be easily frightened makes it almost unbearable. I think again about what he told me earlier, last night it must have been, at Bawley Bay, that her body had disappeared.

"The other watermen think I'm messing around and trying to frighten them – what with the time of year and the stories being spread around. They keep trying to humour me saying that she's probably still in the river, caught on something that's stopping her coming to the surface, but I know otherwise, Miss. As far as the watermen are concerned, two women have been recovered and so that's the end of the matter. But I don't know who that other person is. I'm sorry to say all this to you, Miss."

I can find no words of reply but simply stare at George in astonishment mixed with terror, until I feel my legs weaken and my sight reduce to a small circle of light amongst darkness. On regaining consciousness I am lying in bed once more, but this time Lily, George's wife, is at my bedside, and I can sense that George is hovering, looking uncomfortable and uncertain, filling the entrance to the room.

"You fainted, Miss," Lily advises me in a serious tone. "Have this broth will you Miss Jane? You must regain your strength – you look sadly thin and pale to me."

I take the earthenware bowl and home-made bread that Lily hands me, although the meaty smell, usually so inviting, makes me feel nauseous.

"Thank you, Lily. I am sorry to cause you such trouble."

"Hush now, Miss. Don't you go upsetting yourself. George and I want to help you… especially seeing as how you are in such terrible need at present. We'll do whatever we can. Don't you worry about that."

I do as Lily bids me and struggle to eat as much as I can, because I know that she and George can ill afford to find extra sustenance for me. While I drink the soup I contemplate Lily and wonder how much of this shocking tale George has divulged to his wife. But however much or little she knows, she looks back at me kindly and steadfastly as I eat, and asks nothing of me, other than that I finish the contents of the bowl. Inwardly, I am grateful to her for that too.

After eating I feel recovered enough to rise, despite the protestations of the good and faithful pair. As I do so, I place yet another obligation upon George's shoulders,

"George?"

"Yes, Miss."

"Later this morning I shall place a bundle of papers tied with a pink ribbon in my writing desk. If... if anything should happen to me, if I should be taken anywhere, you must... will you please bring them to me – wherever I am? It is important. I mean... my life may depend on them."

It is a measure of George's character and of our bond that he asks no questions, but simply agrees to comply with my wishes.

My two friends leave after a while saying that they will return later in the day to see how I am faring. I omit to tell them that I do not expect to be here, as I cannot face the distress, both my own and, I like to flatter myself, theirs.

In the silence of the empty room, I resolve, with even greater determination, to document my version of these awful events. I need to prove my innocence and my sanity, both to the superintendent of the asylum, but also, and for this I feel an even greater sense of urgency and desperation, to myself. I sit down at my writing desk, dip my pen in ink and start to write for the second time that morning.

Beginning

Dr Westcott's Study, Stone House, Christmas Eve 1928

Bennett reappeared and poured each of the three gentlemen a generous measure of brandy. He positioned a reading lamp close to Dr Westcott, and stoked the fire. As he left the room, he closed the door as silently as the tumbling snow.

Dr Westcott took a large draught of brandy, turned to his colleagues and, as the firelight cast unsettling shadows around the room, uttered in a low, eerie voice,

"Now then, Gentlemen, as you will hear, Miss Waterford's narrative rests on the truth or otherwise of a series of inexplicable happenings. Therefore, as I have said, I am sure that when you have heard the full account, you will agree with me that it is imperative that these documents are destroyed. That done, we need never speak of them again.

"If you are ready, let us attend to her tale."

Dr Westcott placed the papers on his lap and began reading from the appeal addressed to his father:

Dear Dr Westcott,

If you have this letter before you, then I am already held captive in your asylum. I beg you to consider it in its entirety and conclude that I am a sane and innocent woman. You have been deceived by the

same evil man who has entrapped me. Please…
please… have faith in my exposition and arrange for
my release. The safety of many people depends on the
actions you now take.

My story begins last winter-time – the winter
of 1865.

Winter 1865

My precious memory of the moment I first
encountered Kathryn Lawton is as clear to me now as
the translucent icicle clinging to the snow-encrusted
roofs across the street. Unlike the usually fluid images
of daily life, this impression of her remains captured
and unwavering in my mind as if it too had been
frozen in time. Likewise, I was arrested by her beauty
and the course of my life was altered forever by that
one chance meeting. It was a strange and contrary
circumstance in that I had reached the point in my life
at which I had become reconciled to, maybe even
achieved a degree of acceptance of, what I presumed
would be my fate.

Until that time, I had been living a solitary
existence when I was not helping to educate the
children at the Ragged School in my hometown of
G____, situated beside the River Thames in Kent.
This was mainly because, like Charlotte Brontë's
wonderful character and my partial namesake, Jane
Eyre, I was an orphan. My poor father had passed
away two years earlier and my mother's life had been
taken in childbirth; not by my own arrival in the world,

but by that of a brother who outlived her by only a matter of days. I possessed no further brothers, nor indeed siblings, for whom I was expected to act as housekeeper. Thus, I was deemed to have no womanly role, as I was not called upon to enact the duties of a wife, mother, daughter or sister. Unfortunately, I had little influence over the latter two states and, as for being a wife and mother, they were different issues altogether; marriage and bearing children, it seemed to me, should be a question of personal choice.

They were not for most women, of course. Indeed, many people of the town ostracised me because they regarded me as odd; a superfluous spinster, who had failed in her matrimonial endeavours. This bothered me little. In fact, it made me smile secretly, as I had made no endeavours of which I was aware. I had felt unwilling to settle for marriage and had sought a different life, although over the years I had, of necessity, struggled to come to terms with the certainty (or so I had thought) that this preference would not be attainable. When he died, my father had left me a small annuity upon which I managed to live at a reasonable level of comfort and, as I say, I had become resigned to my secluded way of living. As I sit writing this, how I wish with all my heart that I could return to that undisturbed, if dull, existence!

It is often when we are in such a state of acquiescence that change, both welcome and unwelcome, can leap upon us unexpectedly, like a wild beast. We have ceased to seek it and so it decides to pounce. So it was for me that fateful day. However, I could never have envisaged how vast an upheaval was about to be wrought upon my peaceful existence, stemming from something as insignificant as a transitory look. Upon reflection, I can see that it was an ill-fated glance that initiated an inauspicious sequence of events for us both.

It seems fitting to me now that Kathryn and I first met at the riverside, as that is where I saw her for the final time. So much has happened in the short intervening period that I hardly know where to begin. I say we met, although it was barely that, the first time. The Thames had started to freeze. This was a rare thrill and we, like many others, were drawn to viewing it as moths are lured to a burning flame. As we passed, walking in opposite directions on the promenade, we had no reason to speak, but regarded each other like any two people would. Yet, something occurred that was almost imperceptible, but not quite – not to me at least. There was a moment when our eyes met and we held each other's gaze longer than is considered polite or can be attributed to a mere passing interest or curiosity. It might only have been a fraction of a second, but it seemed to me to be rich with significance. It was a sign that I was only too willing to receive, and both my heart and stomach leapt in response.

I spent the following days in torment. Curiously, I could not determine which would be the greater agony: that I was mistaken and had concocted that sparkle of attraction – of recognition – or that one really had occurred. In the former state of mind, I supposed that she had continued to observe me, purely because I had been so bold in looking at her for that tiny part of a second too long. I can hardly believe that I dared to do it. Conversely, if something unusual *had* happened, would I be strong enough to cope with what that might mean? Either way, I felt as though my senses had been awakened from a long, dull, sluggish sleep. Also, there had been a young gentleman escorting her – why had I chosen to ignore this incontrovertible aspect of the encounter? Surely, he was her *fiancé*, maybe even her husband. He had bowed to me of course, but his forehead has been creased by a deep frown as he did so. Needless to say, he had witnessed the wordless exchange! All in all, my suffering could not have been greater than if I had been on trial at the Old Bailey and waiting to discover whether I was to be publicly hanged outside Newgate Prison. It was not until many weeks later that I had another opportunity to discover on which side of the line my verdict was to fall.

In my solitary condition, my spirits were sustained by a passion for reading, especially novels. It was in indulging that pleasure, usually an insular and unshared activity, which ultimately led me to chance upon Kathryn a second time. My one extravagance, paid for from my annuity, was a subscription to the Literary Institute in H____ Street. I say extravagance, as I am certain many people in this town would have judged it at best a frivolous luxury for a woman of my class (or for any woman of any class for that matter) to have access to such literary treasures. But to me it was an essential lifeline to an imaginary world and one that was at that time, I had to admit, far preferable to the reality of my own.

The day had arrived for my weekly outing to the Literary Institute. It was one of those raw winter days that entice us to remain by the hearth and huddle closer to the roaring fire. A light covering of snow had descended overnight and the freezing temperatures had given rise to a fog that was hanging over the river in dense folds. The river, which was nearly always a silent presence in the town, seemed invisible to the eye and noiseless to the ear. Nevertheless, despite these uninviting conditions, I set out from home as I was determined to seek my regular recreation. The air burned my throat and I lost my foothold on numerous occasions as the pavements were slippery underfoot, but eventually I reached the steps leading up to the entrance of the grand old building.

Once inside, I walked boldly across the hall and into the Reading Room. The presence of women in here was frowned upon generally, and particularly so on certain days of the week. Being of a strong-minded nature, I always ensured that my visits coincided with such prohibited periods. I could not understand what harm I could cause when all I did was sit unobtrusively and read. They would have to ask me to leave outright and they had never done so yet. I took up my usual place at one of the tables and had become deeply engrossed, when I became aware of someone taking possession of the chair on the opposite side of the breadth of dark walnut. I hardly dared to raise my eyes.

I could tell from the rustling of silk finery that it was a woman, and a well-dressed one, but was it her? I chastised myself immediately for the absurdity of this question but, all the same, I could no longer concentrate on the passage I had been attempting to read.

After a while I heard a gentleman's voice, speaking in hushed tones,

"I shall return for you presently, Kathryn, when I have completed my errands and had my appointment with Mr. Stirling at the bank."

When he had ceased talking I sensed, rather than witnessed (as I was keeping my face firmly tilted down into my book) the disapproving scowls of our fellow-readers, but heard the cacophony of 'shushing' more clearly than I would have liked.

"Will you be comfortable here?" he asked doubtfully, in even more of a whisper, to the extent that I had to strain my hearing to catch both his question and her reply, whilst also concealing the fact that I was doing any such thing.

"You know I am passionate about reading, Edward, and I have already seen something that I am interested in perusing. Please do not be concerned and I will wait here for you to return."

As she said this, she motioned her hand towards the latest edition of the local newspaper, the G____ Reporter. She seemed agitated and had discreetly placed her small purchases in such a way that obscured the headline, but I had seen it earlier and knew that it stated baldly, "Tragic Accident at Bawley Bay: Fifty Year Anniversary."

Edward did not seem to notice,

"Well, at least there is another lady present – it strikes me that the natives are somewhat hostile," he mumbled, surveying the room and seemingly only partially reassured.

With that he turned on his heel and was gone from the room. But not before hesitating in front of, and politely nodding to, an ancient gentleman whose habit it was to randomly shout aloud a sentence from his book. As chance would have it, he had just started *Great Expectations*, causing him to bellow in a voice true to Magwitch's own,

"Keep still, you little devil, or I'll cut your throat," in Edward's direction as he approached.

Seeing this, Kathryn smiled faintly and I took the opportunity of her attention being diverted, to consider her. She was as beautiful as I had remembered, although I was surprised to note that an expression of melancholy played about her face. Her colour was ashen too. Perhaps the newspaper headline troubled her – but of what interest could that be to her? Needless to say, I did not dwell on the matter as I had been imagining this moment for many weeks, since our first wordless exchange – what I would say, how I would say it, what I should do. Unfortunately, real-life events seldom present themselves as we might wish, and all my planning was to no avail. I simply stared wide-eyed with disbelief, unable to comprehend that it really was her. The irony of the situation did not pass me by either, as we were in a room in which the Rule of Silence was enforced with an unyielding hand. Any thoughts of communicating had to be firmly suppressed. The undisturbed peace and quiet of the Reading Room was the very nectar that usually drew me to it, but today I could have wailed at the injustice and unreasonableness of such a restriction.

Much to my embarrassment, when Kathryn turned her head away from the direction of Edward's comical departure towards me, I was still staring at her, somewhat intrusively. My facial expression must have been akin to that of a small child unwrapping a much-longed-for gift at Christmas time. I was on the verge of lowering my eyes, in an effort to re-establish my dignity and decorum, when she gazed steadily into them for what seemed an age, before herself becoming absorbed in the front page of the newspaper that had been lying unclaimed on the reading table. I could not determine whether she had recognised me and, as I could feel the blush rising to my cheeks, I felt it safest to do likewise, and returned to my reading matter as if to a place of sanctuary.

But it could not have been otherwise. I was immersed in 'The Moorland Cottage' by Elizabeth Gaskell, my favourite author, and I was fascinated by the relationship between Maggie, the heroine, and Erminia, her close friend since childhood. I had been nearing the climax when Kathryn and Edward had arrived and upon taking it up again I immediately reached the point where Maggie is about to leave home and accompany her errant brother on a sea-voyage to America. I found the scene of her parting from Erminia breath-taking, with Erminia expressing a passionate entreaty for Maggie to abandon the idea of going. Maggie, though, is resolute and the two women say their farewells. To my astonishment I read the words, "Kissing each other, with long, lingering delay, they parted."

I gasped. Instinctively I raised my head to examine Kathryn's pale features – to ascertain whether she had heard my sharp intake of breath. But no, she continued to read. I lowered my eyes to gaze upon her mouth. Her lips were quivering as she soundlessly outlined each word. I wondered what it would feel like to place my mouth upon hers and soothe the trembling. At that moment, she must have suspected that I was studying her, as she stopped and looked directly at me before I had chance to turn away. Our eyes met and I removed my scrutiny from her, only to have my guilty stare captured by a male reader peering eagerly into my face. My heart began to palpitate. Could it be that my thoughts, or worse, my sensations and their cause, were being clandestinely whispered into the ear of every gentleman seated in the room? I searched each face. Had they been whispered into Kathryn's ear? I closed my eyes. I felt an acceleration in the blood's passage around my body until I could bear the pounding no more. I could no longer sit calmly.

Looking back, I am ashamed to say that I decided, rather impulsively, to take flight from the Reading Room and return home, as the feelings being stirred up in me were unfamiliar. Indeed, they were more than I could tolerate. I was aware that Kathryn reacted in surprise at my sudden movement, but I felt unable to return her gaze and kept my head down. However, in my haste and panic I had forgotten that the outside steps of the Literary Institute were covered in a film of ice. Before I knew it, I was sitting on the ground clutching my ankle, which felt as though it must be broken, and proclaiming an oath in an extremely unladylike manner.

Almost immediately, a voice, close to my ear, uttered the words,

"Please, do allow me to assist you. My name is Lawton, Edward Lawton."

It was Kathryn's Edward, returning from his errands sooner than expected. On standing, it became clear to us both that I was unable to walk unaided. He helped me back into the hall of the Literary Institute, secured a chair for me, and instructed me to wait. As I sat there in a helpless state I ruminated on how I hated to be a nuisance to anyone and how I disliked losing my independence even more. But such thoughts soon evaporated as, before long, Kathryn appeared, knelt close at my side, and took my gloved hands in hers.

"Oh, you poor love," she sighed as if she only wanted me to hear and then said more emphatically, still focussing her gaze on me, "Edward, we must take this young lady home with us, as she is not capable of returning to her own residence alone."

But Edward exclaimed, crossly I thought,

"No Kathryn, that is not a good idea at all, with matters the way they are."

His regard was fastened upon our coupled hands and his frown had returned, making his handsome face appear asymmetrical.

Although I had no notion of to what he was referring, part of me felt inclined to agree with him at an instinctual level and I attempted to remonstrate, if rather half-heartedly,

"No, but thank you, I must go home. I will be able to cope perfectly on my own."

In spite of my resolution, on attempting to rise and take a step on my injured ankle, it became clear to me that I was unable to hobble, let alone manage.

Before long I was installed in a spacious suite of rooms on the second floor of a grand house on W____ Hill. The doctor was summoned. Upon examining my ankle, he pronounced that it was not broken, but that I had severely damaged a ligament. He prescribed a week of bed-rest and a small vial of laudanum to be taken daily. When he had left, Kathryn came to my room and gently inquired,

"I am afraid we have few servants here, and so perhaps you would not mind if I nursed you?"

Naturally, in my debilitated condition I had little choice in the matter and so I had to succumb to her wishes. I tried not to show my feelings – a heady concoction of excitement and terror – too freely. It did occur to me that this seemed an odd thing for her to say as, even though I had only been in the house for a short while, a few hours at the most, I had become aware that each room seemed to be whirling with servants attending to their respective duties. However, it suited me to push these thoughts aside and, as I had no experience of how people of the upper class lived, I merely replied, as disinterestedly as I could manage,

"No, I do not mind, if you think it best."

In reply, she gazed into my eyes and smiled,

Needless to say, that week was one of the most joyful of my life. Although I required little in the way of traditional nursing, the arrangement provided us with a great deal of opportunity to spend intimate time together without the intrusion of other members of the household. The only exception was Kathryn's maid, Betty Drummond, who we brought into our confidence.

Even so, I was fearful that we were causing suspicions to be raised, especially Edward's. I kept seeing in my mind's eye the way he had peered so disapprovingly at my hands in Kathryn's when she had come to me in the hall of the Literary Institute. Edward, it transpired, was the young gentleman I had seen with Kathryn on the promenade and, of greater interest to me, turned out to be her older brother. He was highly – I might even say overly – protective of Kathryn in all but the tiniest of concerns. I sensed that, without it appearing unseemly, he desired me to be driven home the instant I was sufficiently recovered.

During that week, Kathryn and I talked of many things and we came to know and like each other's sentiments well. As I grew stronger I also grew bolder, arising I think in part from my emerging feeling of being so comfortable in her presence.

It was at that time that we developed the habit of reading to one another. One evening as I was lying on the couch prior to retiring, I asked her,

"Will you read 'The Moorland Cottage' to me?"

Her countenance betrayed a fleeting gleam of surprise coupled with intense interest, and she reached for the story. When she arrived at the part that had sent me fleeing from the Reading Room, she put the book to one side, leaned over me and kissed me with long, lingering delay. Away from Edward and from the prying eyes of the gentlemen in the Reading Room, it seemed the most natural act in the world. Thankfully, there was no reason for *us* to be parted that night. According to the medical men, as women we are not capable of feeling arousal, other than with the involvement of a man in marriage, of course. Modesty forbids me to say more, but I now know the medical doctors are sorely mistaken.

***

However, it was not long after this blissful night that I became aware of something dark and disturbing slithering beneath the surface of Kathryn's kind and loving demeanour. A few days later I was awoken abruptly by the sound of a woman screaming in terror. It took me a while to realise that it was not part of my own dream and even longer to comprehend that it was Kathryn. Her throat gurgled as she screamed and her arms and legs were thrashing about as though she were fighting with somebody or something. I held her tight and tried my utmost to comfort her,

"My love, what on earth is the matter? There, there, calm yourself. There is nothing to be frightened of – it was just a horrible nightmare."

As she calmed down, her resolve to divulge nothing about her lurid dream strengthened. So, later that day, when Kathryn was occupied with giving instructions to the cook and housekeeper, I sought an interview with Edward. I told him what had occurred that morning with the intention of discovering whether he could illuminate the cause of her distress. In reply, he did not allude to the fact that I had been present when Kathryn awoke, but looked me directly in the eyes and said,

"Miss Lawton has been experiencing dreadful nightmares for many months, maybe even years; I am confounded by the passing of time. She has told me little about them other than she feels she is drowning and it is always in the river, this river I mean, the Thames. I am afraid they are taking their toll on her nerves and her physical strength.

"That was one of the reasons I was reluctant for you to come here... or... or become attached to her. Obviously when she is married, her husband will become her protector and will take care of her," he added looking stern.

"Do you think they are a premonition? I mean, should you not consult a physician?" I interrupted confusedly, feeling extremely perturbed at this revelation, and ignoring his comment about Kathryn's inevitable marriage. I, to this day, do not know what made me ask the first question and I knew that by asking the second I was raising the awful spectre of Kathryn's mind being unbalanced.

"I have done so already," he replied, "but I do not think this is anything our man can cure, if it is anything that can be solved at all. There are just some phenomena, I mean some workings of the female mind, Miss Waterford, that cannot be explained in a rational way. I moved my sister to G____ to get her out of the clutches of someone in London, but I am worried that the proximity of this town to the River Thames has been a terrible mistake for us."

"I cannot understand what you are saying, Mr Lawton. Who? Who is he? Was he a suitor? Please explain more clearly," I implored.

"He? No, I am sorry Miss Waterford, I have disclosed too much already. If you and Miss Lawton are to remain... to remain... er... friends, and she wants you to know more, then she must tell you herself."

And that was that. Neither Edward nor Kathryn ever touched, voluntarily, on the subject again, and I was left to fathom out the mystery for myself based on the gradual unfolding of events that are almost too ghastly to relate.

Arrival

Friday December 14, 1866

Nearly a year had elapsed since Kathryn and I first became acquainted. Winter-time had arrived again and the season was deteriorating into another harsh one. We had enjoyed a wonderful year together and were still passionately in love. I was relishing many new delights. It was true, I had admired women before, but always furtively. I had observed, but no more. I had certainly never felt the joy of falling in love nor of having my sentiments reciprocated. Many people in our society view ardent relationships between unmarried women as Romantic Friendships and, as such, consider them to be acceptable: they are perceived as nothing more than a rehearsal for marriage. Kathryn and I let others believe that that was the true nature of our attachment but, to my mind, our bond was no such thing – no, not for me anyway. It would be inadvisable for me to speak on Kathryn's behalf, but I thought sure she felt the same.

Nonetheless, we could not escape the fact that she and I were of different classes and were confronting dissimilar personal circumstances. Thus, we had conflicting expectations of life. Suffice to say, we faced diverse pressures and constraints imposed by others and Kathryn was clearly expected to marry, and to be wed to a gentleman of her class with satisfactory wealth and prospects. Although I prayed constantly that that abominable day would never arrive, I also knew that its advent was inescapable. Inevitably, this caused me to ruminate upon the remark that Edward had made last winter that there was someone in London who was interested in her – as if she were an artefact to be auctioned at Christie, Manson and Woods – someone whom Edward regarded as utterly unsuitable. Perhaps this man was lurking in wait for her, even now. Perhaps he would pursue her.

In the meantime, Kathryn was inundated with household responsibilities; with attending to Edward and their bed-bound father. However, until this time, she had still devoted plentiful time to me – to us. For my part, I had my teaching and various occupations that kept me engaged. Obviously, it would have been inconceivable for us to live together, but we spent as much time unaccompanied as we could and, if we were not alone, we were with Edward. He venerated us now. He was convinced that we were indulging in an ideal Romantic Friendship, alluding to us on occasion, much to his own delight and amusement, as 'The Ladies of G____.' I think he felt that if he believed it to be true, then so it would be. He would not have been so enthusiastic if he had known the true character of our connection. Nevertheless, with hindsight, I wish we *had* all lived together, as I might have been able to prevent the horrifying chain of events that I will now relate from taking place.

On this particular chilly evening in December when it was nearing dusk, Kathryn and I were strolling by the river later than we had intended. We had ambled arm-in-arm to the end of the Town Pier as from there we could have a fine view of, not only the water, but also the lively sight of the shrimp fishermen setting off for the night in their wonderful bawley boats.

Although fishing was still important to the town, G____ had also become a fashionable tourist destination for wealthy Londoners. As we were about to leave the pier due to the encroaching darkness, one of the regular steamboat ferries arrived bringing a group of well-dressed visitors to our riverside town, presumably for an evening of entertainment. We call this the Long Ferry locally as it is the one that travels up and down the Thames to and from London. This appellation distinguishes it from the short crossing that simply traverses the wide expanse of river to destinations in the county of Essex, such as Tilbury, on the opposite bank. I was about to observe to Kathryn that this particular ferryboat, the *Margery*, was the one on which George usually worked when, discerning that a large crowd was about to disembark, I turned to her whilst pulling her arm with mine and said instead,

"Come Kathryn, let us move out of the path of these revellers and make our way back to W____ Hill. Edward will be wondering where we are."

But she did not appear to hear me, being instead rooted to the ground. Feeling the strength of her resistance, I had unlinked my arm and walked a few steps away. I had assumed that she would follow but, seeing that she and I were now separated, I was forced to fight my way back to her against the tide of people who were, by then, surging onto the pier in high spirits. As I reached her she gripped my wrist with the potency of an iron manacle and uttered in a low, hoarse voice that I hardly recognised,

"Eleanor! It is Eleanor. She has come... My God, she has come here... and on the *Margery*. She said she would... when it was time."

Although she appeared to be saying this more to herself than to me, I could not help but follow the direction of her gaze and realised that she was staring at someone standing in shadow at the bow of the steamer, who was making no effort to leave. The woman seemed to be glowering at her, although in the fading visibility it was difficult to be sure. Again, the poor light of dusk made it hard for me to see her clearly but, from her posture, the way she was bent forward, suggested to me that she was frail and old – extremely old.

I was certain that I had never seen this being before, but I was also struck by a rising feeling of fear, panic even, that she induced in me. A terrible chill rippled slowly through me and slipped across my skin like a jellyfish. I am convinced I felt these sensations at the time rather than ascribing them with hindsight. Admittedly, my terror may have been accentuated by how scared Kathryn had become on seeing her, as though it were a contagion. I studied Kathryn's face and saw that she appeared different: she had become extremely pale and an expression unlike anything I had seen before was transforming her face. Her countenance was worse than I had witnessed during her nightmares.

At that moment, threateningly dark clouds positioned themselves above the river like bullies and it was too murky to see anything greatly, except that the lamps on the pier and the ferry shone brightly by contrast and I could just perceive that the figure had disappeared from where she had been standing. Indeed, she had moved so speedily, allowing for her apparent years, that I was taken aback. Afraid that she was going to come ashore, as surely she must, I turned to Kathryn and said, quite bossily I must confess,

"Come Kathryn, we must return to the house. Edward will be fretful about our whereabouts."

"No Jane," she countered. I remember being surprised at the sharpness and decisiveness of her tone. But then she became vague, and continued, "You go, I must stay here to… I must go to her to…"

As she appeared to be so pre-occupied that she was unable to complete her sentences, I moved away and was conveyed by the flowing throng along the length of the pier towards the High Street; but I did not go home – at least, not straight away. I positioned myself out of sight behind the Tollhouse with the intention of waiting and watching what transpired as soon as the crowd had dispersed. However, almost immediately I was discovered by Edward, who was in no mood to hide his displeasure,

"For goodness sake, Jane, what the deuce is going on? I have been scouring the town for you both. Do you know what time it is? Why are you concealing yourself here in this fashion? Where is Kathryn? Have you abandoned her? In public? Amidst all these strangers?"

I managed to quash the feeling of irritation that, as usual, his over-protectiveness gave rise to, but before I could begin to address each of his myriad questions, he caught sight of Kathryn standing close by the old lady.

By now the situation had become worse in that Kathryn had boarded the ferry as if she intended to return to London with her.

"Good God!" Edward exclaimed in a manner that was quite out of character. Indeed, his whole bearing towards me was unlike his usual calm, polite self.

By now I was feeling exceedingly worried and implored him,

"Edward, please tell me what is going on. I have a right to know. Kathryn and I are... that is, she is my–"

"No Jane, you have no rights, no rights at all!" he interrupted angrily, "Please go home and leave me to deal with this."

"With what? Who is this woman? Who is she?" I asked, feeling increasingly exasperated and desperate.

"Not now Jane, go home," Edward repeated authoritatively, between gritted teeth.

Edward and I had been so submerged in argument that we had not noticed that the steamer had begun to move away from the pier. Upon realising this, he started walking, no running, yelling and waving frantically at the captain to make him stop.

I could not bear to witness more and so turned towards the town.

As I write this, I wonder at my passive obedience to Edward and I would defend myself by saying that it is not my custom to be so compliant. I would never have deserted Kathryn if Edward had not arrived. Although he and I were often in conflict, we were united in our common love for Kathryn, and our desire to shelter her from danger. I knew that I could trust him to protect her with his life. My own trepidation played a part too as I was certain I needed to put a distance between me and that troubling woman. Nevertheless, I returned home reluctantly and I never discovered what occurred between the three of them that night after I had departed.

***

Once there I ate a morsel of supper in silence. I ruminated anxiously over the scenes that I had just witnessed, while attempting to swallow foodstuff with the dry, splintered texture of timber. What were their significance? I had never before seen Edward react in such an inexplicable manner. I was upset too because the evening was ruined. Sitting here alone was a far cry from the intimate dinner that Kathryn and I had been anticipating while Edward attended his chess club. Having said that, my disappointment was a relatively trifling matter, of course. Of greater consequence was my horrible dread of this woman coupled with my anguish about being kept in the dark – by Edward and, indeed, by Kathryn. Who was she and how was she connected to them? Perhaps she was a relation who wanted to tear Kathryn away from my clutches, as she would view it, for the sake of the family name. Could it be that all three were conspiring against me? Although I tried to reassure myself that she was harmless, I could not stop obsessing about whether Edward had been able to rescue Kathryn and, better still, had he managed to persuade the old lady to leave G____?

Yes, if truth be told, I was even doubting Kathryn. I reflected that none of us are really allowed into the past secrets of those we love. A swarm of insecurities erupted on the surface of my being like an outbreak of the smallpox.

I desperately needed a soothing balm. I wanted to take someone into my confidence who was not a member of Kathryn's family, but the real nature of our relationship was invisible to everyone in the town beyond Betty Drummond. I reminded myself that our tie had no enduring status and would have been disapproved of even if it were more widely acknowledged. It was like trying to grasp at smoke and hold it captive in my hand. As I said earlier, I was afraid that people would dismiss it as temporary, as a Romantic Friendship that we were both indulging in until one or both of us experienced true love for a man. I am sure that most gentlemen and ladies who are married do not give this state of affairs a second thought and have no idea how dispiriting it is. I felt completely powerless at this moment of crisis in my life.

Tired to the bone I retired to bed, hoping that this incident was well and truly over. I hoped beyond measure that I would never set eyes on that vexatious individual again.

But I did see the old creature again. She haunted my days and nights after I had witnessed that unhappy reunion on the Town Pier. I think it was only a matter of days, yes, probably just over a week, but by the end of it I could barely recognise myself as the person I had been prior to her arrival.

First Visitation

Saturday December 15, 1866

The next morning a calamity occurred that expunged even these unfathomable affairs from my mind. As a teacher at the school, on occasion, I grew to know and love my pupils' parents as well as the children themselves. One such couple were George and Lily Coombes who, although George worked himself into a perpetual state of exhaustion as a waterman by day and a shrimper by night, lived a life of dire want. George, in the tradition of his father before him, was a proud Thames Waterman – a Freeman of 'The Company of Watermen and Lightermen of the River Thames,' to give his official title. Although poor, he was adamant that his son, Peter, should be educated so that he was provided with the best chance in life. George thought that everyone deserved that. He also held the view that every person, whether man or woman, should be free to live as they saw fit and, I am pleased to say, that included me. Lily, who had been raised in the local workhouse, had recently given birth to their second child, a beautiful boy named Joe, but she was struggling to cope due to her own poor health.

We had all become close since I had acted as an inexperienced midwife at the birth and so I was aware that the baby was underweight and ailing. Even worse, marsh fever was a constant threat to the inhabitants of our riverside town and I knew that Lily had seen enough of it in the workhouse to recognise the symptoms and understand their gravity. At about five o'clock that morning George hurried over to tell me that Joe had become gravely ill during the night and that Lily was desperately worried. Without a moment's hesitation I told George to go on ahead and I would follow him as quickly as I could.

It was piercingly cold as I left home and the town was enveloped in that pre-dawn darkness that only a still winter's morning can bring. George and Lily lived in Slaves Alley, a poverty-stricken district of G___, and my quickest route by far to this neighbourhood was one that took me along the river.

I had no sooner arrived at the water's edge than I wished I had not been so hasty in sending George away, but had rather asked him to wait and escort me. I felt that the scene had a threatening quality as all seemed unnervingly silent, quite unlike I had ever experienced during the daytime. This was partly because it was low-tide and both the river and the shoreline were deserted of the lively industry of the Thames watermen and fishermen. Also, the water, which usually lapped energetically at the shore, was eerily motionless. The sole sound was the slow, rhythmic moaning from the dark, spectral forms of the unpeopled boats resting on the water. But it was the all-consuming darkness that evoked a terrible feeling of apprehension in me. I was being devoured by anxiety which was gnawing at the pit of my stomach. I chided myself saying that it was simply a question of my not being accustomed to visiting this setting before daybreak; that was all. I attempted to pull myself together or, I told myself, if I could not do that, at least I should start moving as George and Lily would be waiting anxiously for me.

I found my way cautiously along the rough bank of the river and before long I was level with the Town Pier, the site of last evening's mysterious encounter. I glanced towards the end of the pier, which stretched out into the gloomy, empty waters of the river. I was absent-mindedly thinking how relieved I was that the old woman (Eleanor was it that Kathryn had called her?) would no longer be in the vicinity, when I realised, to my horror, that she *was* here – at the far end of the pier. The lamps of the pier were still aflame and I could see her illuminated amidst the darkness like a solitary warning beacon. However, she had not seen me, as it was not me that she was seeking. She appeared to be draped over the side railings of the pier like a tangle of discarded fishing nets, searching intently for something in the river. Although I know now what it was, I did not know then. Had I known, I would have turned and run as fast as my utterly restrictive garments would allow.

As it was, I felt sympathy for her. I was moved by the vision of such an aged mortal looking hopelessly into the river at such an inhospitable hour in the morning and in such bitter winter weather. I realised too that, last night, I had not noticed her attire (probably because I had not been able to see her clearly), but this morning I could see that she was clothed in a mode of dress that was wholly unfamiliar to me. Indeed, her costume appeared so old-fashioned that it too evoked my pity in a peculiar sort of way but, more than that, it gave her the disturbing appearance of a visitor from… from… the past. Her raiment was out of keeping with her age too – it was appropriate to a much younger woman. Yet again, the sight of her unsettled me. I was torn in my loyalties as I knew that George and Lily needed me, but at least they had each other – I believed I was needed here too.

I decided to approach Eleanor and so I started to walk tentatively along the pier, becoming intensely aware of the swirling water visible beneath my feet as I did so. The river was now moving quickly due to the turning tide and its smooth flow was impeded by the struts of the pier. Consequently, its constant circular motion was making me feel giddy, as though enticing me towards its icy depths. I lunged to my left and grabbed hold of the railings to steady myself. I walked on. Despite the echoing noise that my shoes were making on the cast-iron slats, Eleanor seemed to remain oblivious of my presence until I had traversed over three-quarters of the pier's length. When I reached this point, by which time I was standing close to her, she suddenly reacted and, turning in my direction, glared at me with an expression, the like of which I had never before seen on another person's face, nor indeed have I since. It was full of such abhorrence that I wondered whether, indeed, we *had* met before, if not in this life, then perhaps in another. At that moment, I felt certain that *she knew me*, even if she were a stranger to me. I felt the same sensation of cold shudders surging throughout my body as I had the previous evening. I started to shake uncontrollably and my heart began pulsating when it suddenly occurred to me that, on this occasion, I was completely alone with her.

But still she said nothing and gradually I realised that she was glaring past me at a point just above my right shoulder. She was so fixed upon this perspective that I was desperate to turn around to see who it was that must surely be standing behind me. Perhaps I had been so intent on making my tentative way along the pier like a sea-sick voyager that I had been unaware of someone doing the identical thing, noiselessly behind me. If so, I was trapped at the end of the pier between this soul and Eleanor, high above the deep, churning waters. But, even so, I was too terrified to turn my back on her. My eyes were fastened on her features as I witnessed her gasp and then sob, but still I could not bring myself to look. To my mind, whoever was there could not pose more of a threat to me than this creature standing before me.

After a period of silence that seemed interminable, I gathered my courage and asked with a voice that I knew was faint with fear,

"It is Mrs... I mean... Eleanor is it not?" I was forced to dispense with formalities as I was ignorant of her surname and she clearly was not going to assist me by offering it to me.

Still she gave no verbal response, but continued to direct her evil glare in my direction.

"Have you let something fall into the river?"

No reply.

Then my questions came thick and fast and I left no pauses for her answers, as my anxiety intensified,

"Are you in distress?"

"Can I do anything to help?"

"Would you like me to fetch some warmer clothing for you?"

Eventually, as she failed to answer any of my enquiries, I became quiet and simply watched her, waiting impatiently for her to speak. Yet, still she remained mute and continued to look beyond me in that terrible manner. I could no longer resist my compulsion. I glanced behind but... but... nobody was there.

In the next moment, something happened that I could not account for then and cannot account for now... other than... As everyone in this town knows, a pier has a clear purpose which is simply to allow people to embark onto or disembark from boats that are too large to traverse the shallower waters near the shore. Once the end of a pier is reached, there are only two ways in which a person can leave it safely: they must either climb onto a vessel or return the way they have come by walking back along its length. But that morning, Eleanor took neither of these routes – there was no steamer moored alongside the pier and she did not pass by me. Instead, I watched in a paralysis of panic as her body suddenly contorted and swayed, her uplifted arms pushed and pulled, as if she were wrestling against someone. If it were so, I could not see them. Then suddenly, to my horror, before I could react, she bent forward over the railings and plummeted headlong into the deep, freezing river.

Naturally, at the time, I could give no coherent explanation for her apparent struggle with the phantom menace, nor could I account for two perplexing conundrums that tortured me – *she did not scream and, far, far more disturbing, I did not hear a splash as her body entered the water, as surely it must have done.* They still torment me, even though – no because – I know now for sure. Instinctively, upon seeing her fall, I screamed as hard as my lungs would allow and dashed to the position from which she had vanished. I scrutinised the waters below, but there was no evidence of her. There was not even any disturbance to the water, let alone a woman flailing about. I had never learnt to swim and so I knew that following her into the river would be pointless, especially in such icy temperatures. Besides, how could I be certain that she was in the water?

I looked around desperately for someone to assist me, either on land or in a boat, but there was no-one. Left alone at the end of the pier, it struck me with horror that had anyone seen me, I must have taken on the likeness of Eleanor herself, as she had appeared when I found her, while I peered searchingly into the water. I felt terrified that I might have unwittingly entered into an uncanny cycle of happenings that were destined to repeat themselves no matter what action I now took.

I stayed grasping the rail until my fingers became numb despite the thickness of my gloves and I could hardly draw breath. I started choking and, for a while, had an overwhelming sensation that I too were drowning; that my windpipe and lungs were filling up with filthy, brown river water. At the time I assumed my body was suffering from the effect of my sheer terror at what I had witnessed, or that it was due to a fear that I might be the next victim of whoever had caused Eleanor to fall. But, as far as I could tell, I was left totally alone. I felt utterly bewildered.

***

Looking back, I am shocked to admit how easily the mind can be deceived into dismissing out of hand portents that cannot be comprehended. At that moment I convinced myself that I had imagined it all and, although badly shaken, since nothing else transpired, I resumed my journey to George and Lily's home. Outwardly, I spent the day immersed in helping Lily nurse the sick baby, allowing her to take some well-needed rest. I refrained from divulging to George and Lily anything concerning what had occurred with Eleanor, as I felt that they already had enough distress to cope with. By the end of the day, although little Joe was still very ill, he had not deteriorated significantly and so I decided to return home. With hindsight, my decision to leave them seems somewhat selfish and uncaring and is one that I bitterly regret. However, I needed time to think about the unnerving occurrence on the pier, and to decide what, if anything, I was going to do about it.

As I am sure you can appreciate, all through the day I had revisited the startling episode time and time again in my mind and tried to persuade myself that it had all been a trick of the lamplights and the swaying shadows they cast. As I say, I did not discuss the incident with George or Lily and indeed, I did not feel that I could talk to anyone about what I had seen, or at least, what I thought I had seen. As a result, I was left alone, imprisoned even, with my own uncertainties and sense of foreboding. Was I going mad? Had I been hallucinating? If not, how could I account for it? I felt all the more determined that I needed to know who this… this… woman was and, more importantly to me, what was her association with Kathryn. What did she want from her?

As night fell, I felt more and more agitated and resolved that I must talk to Kathryn about what I had seen. When I arrived at the house and was shown into the drawing room, I found her sitting quietly in the half-light and seeming troubled, with her sewing on her lap, untouched. No candles were lit. She turned to face me and, from her expression, I sensed, for the first time since we had become intimate, that she was not overjoyed by my unexpected arrival. I experienced a sinking feeling and felt my confidence ebb away.

It seemed that Eleanor's coming had changed everything.

Nevertheless, I recounted the mystifying vision to her, but doing so roused my feelings of desperation further, especially when I realised that my words were causing a manifestation of dread to become evident upon her face. She looked down at her sewing in an attempt to conceal her expression. The instant I had finished relating my experience, I demanded,

"Kathryn, please tell me that you can provide an explanation for what I witnessed this morning and… and for last evening."

There followed a long silence as I awaited her reaction, fully expecting her (naively, as I can now perceive) to provide a logical elucidation that satisfied me and for that to be the end of the matter. Her reply, when it came, was both evasive and defensive and it shook me to the core of my being. She had reassembled her face to display a stony expression and replied in an accusatory fashion,

"I think you are jealous, Jane. You are resentful that I chose to spend time with someone other than yourself. It is intolerable – quite suffocating. I fear you have made up the entire incident to prejudice me against Eleanor who, by the way, is simply an acquaintance of my late grandmother. Not that it is really any concern of yours."

I was mortified by her words. Was I really such an ogre? Was I jealous? Certainly, I had not neatly packaged all my anxieties and questions into a box with *that* label adhered to the outside. Indeed, the thought of that particular green-eyed monster had not occurred to me. Why should it?

It is difficult to write this, but I did not believe *her* either. I thought it more likely that Eleanor had something to do with the mysterious suitor that Edward had mentioned last year. Was Eleanor scheming to convince Kathryn to marry this man whom Edward regarded as unsuitable? I fancied that Edward resented the opposition to his authority that Eleanor, as a senior member of the family, represented. She was an aunt... yes, an aged aunt – their mother's older sister, perhaps. Suppose Edward had forced Kathryn to move to G____ against her will and his compulsive over-protectiveness was driving him to shield Kathryn from what he perceived as Eleanor's interference? That might explain his overreaction to her last night. It would be reasonable to presume that Kathryn would want to keep all this from me. However, it would not explain what had occurred this morning.

As I was not certain in my own mind whether this bizarre sighting on the pier had actually taken place, I decided not to challenge Kathryn directly, but to approach the issue from a different perspective. For the second time that day, I found myself asking question after question with the vague notion that, if Kathryn was unwilling to answer them, my interrogation would expose the fact that she was lying. As with Eleanor though, I did not allow Kathryn time to respond and became increasingly aware that I was sounding hysterical,

"When did you last see her? Why has she come here? Why now? Why did you say she would come when it was time? Time for what? Why is her dress so outmoded? For goodness sake, Kathryn, who *is* she, really?"

"I do not wish to discuss this with you any further," she interrupted icily. As if that attempt to terminate the conversation were not outrageous enough, she also changed the topic,

"I do not understand why you waste your time propping up those wretched Coombes people anyway. You are giving yourself a life-sentence helping paupers like that."

I was scandalised. She had never made such an insulting remark concerning my dear friends George and Lily before and, although I had occasionally witnessed her using a hostile tone of voice with the housekeeper, she had never addressed me in such a manner – until now. Perhaps I did not know her after all. At the time, I was so upset by the fact that we were having our first serious disagreement that, holding back tears of both frustration and sadness as well as I could, I left her abruptly with no word of goodbye, no farewell embrace or kiss. As I write this, how I wish I could re-live that parting moment.

Burial

Sunday December 16, 1866

Not surprisingly I tossed and turned for most of the night despite my utter exhaustion after such a distressing day. I could not resist dissecting both my quarrel with Kathryn and the question of whether I should report what I had seen on the Town Pier to someone in authority. They were both itchy scabs that I was compelled to make bleed rather than leave alone to heal in time without scarring. Although these happenings were extremely unsettling, and despite our conversation last night, I tried desperately to reassure myself that my relationship with Kathryn was a trusting one and that she would provide me with a perfectly valid explanation in good time.

I felt far less calm about the other matter. If I did give a statement to the town policeman, what should I say? Surely any sane person would conclude that I was deranged and I would be putting myself at risk of being dragged off to the asylum. On the other hand, what if Eleanor's body washed up at Bawley Bay and it became known that I had witnessed her fall into the river but had told nobody? How could I live with myself? How could I cope with the public humiliation of being thought so dishonest, of failing to raise the alarm at the time of the shocking accident, or within a reasonable interlude? It was already too late for the latter, of course, as a whole day and much of the night had already passed. Even worse, if someone had seen her struggle with her invisible attacker and had seen me close by, perhaps they would accuse *me* of forcing her into the water... *accuse me of causing her to drown! I would be accused of murder!*

Finally, despite these terrible anxieties twisting my intestines into a knot, I sank into a deep but agitated slumber just as the pale light of dawn was seeping into my chamber. But then, of course, I slept for far too long, and did not awaken until a little before eleven o'clock. I stood in front of the looking-glass examining my pallid face fretfully, noticing how agony and terror were altering it, as the bruises under my eyes deepened. Suddenly, the bells of Saint George's Church started to toll mournfully, calling the faithful to Sunday morning worship. The unexpected clangour jolted me out of my sorrowful reverie and I remembered that I had promised to spend another day helping Lily to nurse little Joe. Of necessity I would have to seek my religious sustenance later in the day. Yesterday's only silver lining was that Joe's health had seemed to become more stable as the day had worn on and I fully expected to discover that this had continued during the night; although I knew that nothing could be certain with such a newly born babe, and such a delicate one at that.

If I had not slept so late I would have taken the longer route to George and Lily's abode so that I could avoid the waterfront, as I did not want to be subjected to a further unfathomable encounter with Eleanor. As it was, I was so concerned about the lateness of the hour that I had no choice – I would have to take the risk. At least it was daylight and it was one of those beautiful clear winter's days when the low sun is shining down from a deep blue sky. It felt like the sort of day when nothing unpleasant or upsetting could possibly occur.

As I approached the Town Pier I was taken aback by how the brilliant hue of the sky was reflected in the water, causing it to glisten. The river flaunted a fascinating mixture of azure and emerald green, instead of its usual shades of dull, muddy browns and greys – and so, despite my need to hurry, I stopped to marvel. I had checked the entire length of the pier and had reassured myself that, on this occasion at least, Eleanor was not there.

I hardly had time to relax and allow the relief to wash over me, when I saw something, something vaguely spherical that I could not make sense of in the river – at exactly the point where she had plunged in yesterday. Surely it must be a buoy tied to a fishing boat? But it looked too small and of the incorrect colour and the wrong substance. I strained my eyesight against the bright sunlight and saw… no… no… it cannot be… I shall never forget that moment for as long as I live… I saw, to my horror, that it *was* her. *But, horror of horrors, only a head was visible, as if detached from her body and bobbing on the surface of the water*! How could any woman stay so motionless in the water without sinking out of sight? As yesterday, she seemed to be searching for something but, if anything, her searching was more frantic. After a while the eyes of the head were raised and once again fixed me with a malevolent stare or, at least, so it felt. I heard a series of distant sobs. After a while, I realised that they had come from my own throat.

I had lived in the town since birth and I knew that at the point at which Eleanor was positioned, level with the far end of the pier, the river water was so deep that a person standing on the riverbed would be totally submerged. Even at low tide, no part of them would be visible. That was the whole point of the pier. Even so, a series of rational explanations forced themselves into my mind, as I endeavoured to calm my rising terror. Maybe she was standing on something connected to the structure of the pier. Maybe she was supported by a rowing boat that I was unable to see from my vantage point. Maybe the tide had gone out further than normal so that the river was much shallower than usual. But if truth be told, I was unconvinced by any of these desperate explanations and alarm seared through me.

Instinctively I started to flee, not caring how unladylike I would look to anyone who observed me. My panic escalated further as the rigidity of my corset and the cumbersomeness of my morning gown impeded my movements. Obviously I had no patience with the fashion for tight-lacing, but even so… Consequently, my progress was woefully slow. What if she gave chase and caught me? Fearing this, I turned around repeatedly as I was certain of being pursued, and this made my advancement slower still. Indeed, I stumbled and fell clumsily to the rough surface on two occasions. Once on the ground I could barely right myself. I must have had the appearance of a turtle trapped on its back with its appendages catching helplessly at the air. Such indignity was humiliating! But again, each time I looked apprehensively back towards the pier I received confirmation that I was completely alone. Neither Eleanor, nor anybody else, had chased me or caught up with me. Notwithstanding, I ran and ran until I arrived at George and Lily's door, believing that my hat, hair and garments were in such disarray that I would be impelled to tell them the whole story at last. However, in the circumstances, this was not the case.

I hammered on the dilapidated cellar door, which served as their front entrance and, as George let me in, I knew straight away from the strained expression on his ashen face and from the solemn, if almost imperceptible, shake of his head that little Joe was dead. My hands flew to cover the lower part of my face while my stomach heaved. It took all my resolve not to simply collapse onto the threadbare matting. I felt that I had let them all down dreadfully and this was made worse by the knowledge that I could not tell them why I had arrived so late – too late. Not yet, at least.

I could hear Lily weeping at the rear of the house and went to her without speaking – what use were words at such a time? I put my arms around her, while George and my little pupil, Peter, stood stiffly, looking on. They both looked desolate, but too manly to let their tears flow. My embrace caused Lily to sob long and hard, and she clung to me as she wailed,

"My poor, poor baby boy. He wasn't strong enough for this world…"

I drew upon all my resources, and more, so that I could both calm myself and soothe her distress,

"There, there Lily."

"Oh Miss Jane, thank you, thank you so much for coming to us at this time of our terrible suffering. It is all over for my poor baby. My poor, poor, baby boy."

"Yes, I know, I know. There now."

"What are we going to do without him? What will we do?"

I tried to quieten and comfort her as best I could. In many ways I would have found it more bearable had Lily howled and screamed at me, instead of offering me her gratitude, as if she deserved no better treatment. However, that was not her placid way, and so we sat and wept together. I rocked her gently and, after a while, when she had fallen into a slumber, I rose and approached the makeshift cot. He had been such a dear little thing with a miniature version of George's face, but it had not been his destiny to dwell long on this earth. When I leant over and kissed Joe's cheek, I realised that it was cold and that he had must have been dead for a number of hours. It was time to lay out his little body and make preparations for his burial. This I did, noiselessly and without fuss, whilst George comforted Peter to the best of his abilities.

A couple of hours later I left the family to give vent to their grief in private and commenced my journey home, understandably full of dread concerning what I might encounter along the way. But I could never have been prepared for what occurred. By now it was early afternoon and the brightness that I had experienced as I walked to George and Lily's home was still evident. The light and the enhanced colours around me were in sharp contrast to the misfortune I had just witnessed in that dark home where the nourishing sun's rays never seemed to penetrate. I knew that it was madness to walk along the river, but the prospect of creeping through the claustrophobic town with its shady, narrow streets lined with intimidating buildings was too difficult to bear. Forgetting it was Sunday, I reasoned that, as I was not in the mood for making polite conversation with acquaintances or neighbours and, as I was more likely to meet them amongst the shops, I would be better off walking by the river.

I had not been stumbling along the riverside for long when I heard the distant but unmistakeable sound of the steamboat ferry, presumably making the return journey to London. It was coming from behind and so, although it was not visible to me as I walked in the direction of my home, such a familiar noise was comforting, causing my spirits to lift. As the slapping of the paddle-wheels drew level I instinctively turned around to see if George was working on it (which of course he would not have been that day), as it was our custom to wave to each other on such occasions. But, to my horror, I realised that there was no ferry there – nor indeed, any other boat. I had no sooner been capsized by the shock of this when all at once I heard the terrible sound of a woman screaming. No, she was not solely screaming, she was shrieking a man's name – William, was it? I was unsure. This pitiful sound was followed immediately by a splash as something heavy – yes... as heavy as a human body – fell into the river. Immediately men started shouting and there was a deafening screech of steam being forced out through the steamer's funnel. Then the ferry's paddles simply stopped turning, leaving a dreadful, eerie silence. A silence that was not broken again for as long as I stood there, frozen in horror – looking, no... no... searching, searching in the water – and I stood there alone for an interminable length of time, until I could bear it no longer and dragged myself back to the safety of home.

Once home I paced about, unable to settle to anything, although there was so much I should have been doing. Eventually I sat and drank some tea, but my hands shook terribly and the brown liquid spilled and stained my dress. As I glared at the soiled material I realised that things had progressed too far. I felt as though I were losing the balance of my mind. I could no longer deny the nature of these visitations nor cope with them alone. I needed help and so I resolved to confide in George as soon as possible. I chose George as I knew Edward would be unwilling to discuss them. Although I could barely manage it, I also knew that I would have to wait until after baby Joe had been laid to rest.

Tuesday December 18, 1866

George and Lily wanted me to be present at the burial but, understandably, the ordeal of standing in a graveyard after everything that had happened during the last few days was almost too much to contemplate.

However, after two more nights which were totally devoid of sleep, the wretched day arrived and Joe's minute coffin was lowered into a rough pauper's grave with George, Lily and myself bearing miserable witness. I could not let them down again by not being in attendance, but how I wish I had been able to pay for a decent interment and for Joe to have his own headstone. At least he was enfolded within the sanctity of the church graveyard – I had made sure of that. Not everyone is afforded that blessing. As the rain fell, I steeled myself and prepared for the worst – for Eleanor to appear, I mean – but nothing untoward happened. However, I was increasingly aware that I was starting to resemble a spectre myself as a consequence of my terror and lack of sustaining rest.

Wednesday December 19, 1866

Naturally, I did not want to talk to George about my distressing troubles in the presence of Lily and Peter and so the following day I waited on the river bank, close to the Town Pier, at the time when I knew he would finish his work on the ferry. As he approached he turned pale and his brow furrowed, imagining that I came with further bad news,

"Hello Miss, don't say there's more trouble to bear? Is it Lily? Don't say it's Peter, Miss, I couldn't bear it."

I shook my head in response and reassured him that as far as I knew both were well, and that was not why I had come. When I saw that he was calmer, although he continued to scrutinise me, I embarked on my unnerving tale. I told him of Edward and Kathryn's reaction to seeing Eleanor arrive on the evening ferry last Friday and described Eleanor's subsequent hauntings of me. Firstly, I described my terrifying experience of seeing her on the Town Pier; how she had struggled with an invisible attacker before falling or being forced into the watery depths without trace. I explained how, the next morning, despite her fall, I had witnessed her – or her head – in the very same location in the water. Finally, I related the most recent terror involving the ghostly ferry, the woman's screams, the alarming thud of a body falling into the river, the watermen's cries and the ensuing terrible silence. I also told him how afraid and disturbed I had felt on first seeing Eleanor, although I carefully did not mention my relationship with Kathryn, nor the fact that we were estranged.

When I had finished relating my awful tale, George looked at me steadily with wide eyes. He was unable to hide how shocked he felt, although I was unsure whether this was due to him being worried for my sanity or because he *did* believe what I was telling him. After what seemed like a long pause, speaking in a low voice, he said,

"Would it help you, Miss, if I kept a look out? I can watch out for this being, and I can also take care of Miss Lawton if she travels on the ferry. I know Miss Lawton's important to you, Miss."

"Oh, yes please, George, it would put my mind at rest," I said.

As soon as I had said these words I averted my eyes because I realised that George's promised reports would have the opposite effect on my peace of mind. But, deep down I was encouraged as I had felt sure that George would not disappoint me, that he would be loyal, and it felt such a relief to discover that he knew about my relationship with Kathryn despite all my painful and pitiful attempts at secrecy.

"I can't stay now Miss, as I need to get home to Lily and my little boy," he continued, "but there is something I need to tell you. Can we meet tomorrow evening when I've got more time and I can tell Lily to expect me later than usual? She'll worry if I don't get back now – she's in a bad way still, as you can imagine, Miss."

Having agreed to meet at 8 o'clock the next evening in the school after my class had finished, we went our separate ways.

Christmas Eve 1815

Thursday December 20, 1866

The next evening George and I met at the Ragged School as arranged. He entered the classroom after the children had left and took a seat wearily in the middle of the battered miniature bench that the pupils used. He moved aside a slate writing board and chalk before placing his arms on the desk and facing me as I leaned forward in my teacher's chair at the front. We both contemplated each other in silence for a few seconds and, having taken a deep breath, he commenced,

"I've never told you this before, Miss, as I didn't want to frighten you, but a few weeks ago we, the watermen that is, were chatting about how two women had drowned in the river here after falling from the last steamboat ferry... I mean the last one to leave here on Christmas Eve, in 1815. You probably read about the tragedy in the local paper last year as fifty years had passed since it happened. It was the ferry I work on you see, Miss, the *Margery*."

"Yes, I had heard about the drownings, but I... I did not realise that the women had been travelling on the *Margery*," I stammered, thinking of that awful evening less than a week ago when Eleanor had arrived in G____ on that same ferryboat. I recalled that Kathryn had remarked in horror on the name. I tried to remain calm despite my churning insides.

"Yes, George," I continued, "I saw the headline in the G____ Reporter last winter too, but at the time I could not bring myself to read the article."

I refrained from explaining why I had not read it, as my stomach had lurched again at his words – this time for a different reason. My thoughts had flown to *that* memorable visit to the Literary Institute when Kathryn and I had sat in the Reading Room in each other's company, still strangers but deliciously attracted to one another and delightfully aware of each other's presence. Oh, how I missed her. But his words also prompted me to remember that she *had* seemed overly interested in the piece and that I had been vaguely intrigued by her curiosity. Strangely, Kathryn and I had never discussed it. I let George assume that I had found the prospect of reading it too upsetting whereas, in reality, I confess I had not given the catastrophe another thought since that time as, until recently, so many wonderful things had been happening in my life.

Although I had not read the report, obviously the tragedy was part of the folklore of the town and it would have been impossible to live here for as long as I had without being aware of it. But hearing George allude to the accident as if it had some connection with recent frightening events was disturbing. Even worse, I felt chilled by the idea that there may be some association, however vague or distant, between it and my beautiful Kathryn.

"But how could the calamity be linked with this dreadful woman, Eleanor... or... or... with

Kathryn? She... Miss Lawton... I mean... surely *she* is not in any danger?"

My mind had leapt ahead and I blurted all my tangled thoughts out loud, feeling as though I was losing my self-control.

"Well, Miss, that's what we need to think about. Nobody knows what happened to the women – what, or who, caused them to go overboard, I mean – but what the paper didn't say is that one woman's body was never recovered. The mystery was never cleared up to the satisfaction of the Company men at the time either – some of us are descendants, you see, and the story has been passed down the generations. Some have doubted that it was an accident at all, Miss. My old dad for one."

George looked about him to make sure no-one had crept unnoticed into the room and then whispered,

"But Miss, did you know there is a rumour that the ghost of the missing woman haunts the Thames at G____, especially on the Town Pier and in the waters surrounding it?"

Then, upon seeing the horrified expression on my face as I shook my head, he added,

"But that may just be silly old wives' tales, Miss. No-one said that they have ever actually seen her."

"No... no it is not, George!" I uttered slowly. "That must be who I am seeing! I am being plagued by the ghost of one of the women who died in the accident!"

I had expected George to contradict me, to laugh and tell me that I was mad, but he did not. Instead, he stunned me by replying,

"Yes, I'm afraid I think so, Miss, if I'm honest."

I could feel myself becoming breathless as the terror rose in my chest. I was developing a throbbing headache as a new question pounded my brain: if both women had drowned and Eleanor is the phantom of one of them, then who or what is Kathryn? My beautiful Kathryn… Oh, surely not?

In spite of this thought, I tried to calm down,

"I must find out more, George. Neither Mr Lawton nor Miss Lawton will discuss these mysterious happenings with me. At least, when we talk, I feel they are concealing things from me. I feel as though both my and Miss Lawton's lives depend upon discovering the truth, and my sanity certainly does."

"Well, I'm afraid there *is* more Miss, and I might as well get it out in the open and then we can view it from all angles."

"Please continue," I breathed as my heart beat even faster.

George's face darkened and he spoke faintly,

"On Christmas Eve every year since the awful tragedy, the men working on the last ferry of the evening – if it's the *Margery*, that is – return to their wives and children with ashen, haggard faces. It's a poor Christmas day they spend too because they don't want to frighten their families by saying what's gone on, although the womenfolk sense something terrible has happened. Only on the day after can they relate their awful story to the other watermen.

"That's when I first heard about it Miss, just after last Christmas time. The story the men gave is this: just after the ferry left the Town Pier and entered deep waters they heard a woman screaming at the stern, and so they rushed to where the shrieks were coming from but, seeing as it was so cold, when the men got there they found no one up top. While one of the men dashed to look overboard, the strangest thing happened: unlike the newspaper report, he heard not two, but only one body enter the water. He yelled 'Man Overboard!' the ferry blew off steam and then there was silence. They said it was an eerie silence, just like you described, Miss. Even more disturbing was that, although they had heard it all as clear as a ship's bell, there was nothing to see. It's the tragedy all over again, Miss. Although some say it's a warning of what's to come – because it's different, I mean – the one body going over, not two. Nobody wants to work that shift, Miss, but we must, the ferry must go back to London that evening."

"Oh George," I stifled a sob, "It is exactly the same as I witnessed on Sunday – the day little Joe died – the same terrible sounds, in the same sequence."

"Yes… yes, I know Miss."

"But why are the men talking to you about it now?" I asked. "Have any of them seen anything?"

I tried not to sound panic-stricken although fear was rising in me. I clutched the edge of my desk so forcefully that pain coursed through my fingers.

"Not that I know of, Miss. But I'll ask around. I expect they've spoken about it because the dreaded time is looming again, Miss. We're all getting edgy. I've taken note of their words as I'm going to have to do the shift this year."

"Oh George. Could you not leave it to one of the other crew this time? I mean... for Lily and Peter's sake? After everything you have all suffered?" I added, as I did not want him to think I was questioning his bravery.

"No, Miss. Some poor soul has to do it and we all have to take our turn... like it or no. Besides it'll give me a chance to find out what I can for you, Miss."

"Oh George, thank you, you are a good friend to me," I said with feeling. Then, after a while, something else occurred to me,

"George?" I asked tremulously.

"Yes, Miss."

"Did... did any of the watermen say what either of the women were called?" I asked in a low voice, almost too frightened to pose the question.

"The only name I heard mentioned was Ashburton, Miss, but that means nothing to me at the present time. Does it to you?"

"No... no... George. Neither does it to me."

"Can I make a suggestion, Miss?"

"Yes, go on."

"Please stay away from the river for now, especially the Town Pier, or at least I'll come with you if you do need to go near it... just in case."

I nodded... unable to speak another word. The idea that the terrible accounts George had just given me might be a premonition, another dreadful disaster yet to take place, was too awful to envisage. Especially when coupled with my knowledge of Kathryn's recurring nightmares about drowning in the Thames. If she was in danger, then I had to save her. I would need evidence though, to make her trust in me.

So, after George and I had parted, I resolved to return to the Literary Institute the next day to examine the newspaper article and discover whether it would reveal any further clues.

Friday December 21, 1866

I was waiting outside the building when the doors were unfastened for the day by a stuffy-looking man in uniform. He inspected me with disdain as if I were something messy that he had accidently stepped in and which was obstinately clinging to the underside of his shining black shoes. Once inside, things became no better. Although I paid my annual subscription to the Literary Institute in a timely fashion and with pounds Stirling that were as good as any gentleman's, many hours passed during which obstacle after obstacle was strewn across my path, preventing me from gaining sight of the article. The most obstructive impediment was offered by a diminutive man wearing spherical spectacles peering out from behind a large counter,

"Women cannot request back-copies of newspapers," he announced emphatically, continuing in the same tone,

"You will have to ask your husband to make the request on your behalf. There is a fee, you see."

My response of "I do not possess a husband" was met with a shrug, a look of distaste, and a turning away to more important matters.

In the end I became so frantic that I used deceptive means. I tricked Edward into requesting it for me. When I say tricked I simply mean that I was not totally honest with him about what the newspaper contained and why I wanted it. I think he knew that there was something significant in what I was doing, but he was clearly ignorant of my motive. He disguised his intrigue by pretending to be amused by what he took to be my feminine whim.

Finally, after many wasted hours, the weekly that I was so desperate to read was placed in my outstretched, grasping hands. I hurried into the Reading Room, sat down with the paper on the table in front of me, and read the headline. It was just as I remembered it: "Tragic Accident at Bawley Bay: Fifty Year Anniversary."

I raced through the front page until towards the end I read:

The two women, who both resided in the Chelsea district of London, were named as Mrs W. J. Ashburton (26) and Mrs Kathryn Lawton (25).

I gasped at the second name. My breathing became quick and shallow and, for a while, I felt as though I were about to swoon. But thankfully I recovered. I comforted myself with the thought that no-one's name is unique; it is nothing more than a pure coincidence. I expect there are many other Jane Waterford's inhaling air across the country at this very minute for that matter, completely unrelated to me. It means nothing... nothing at all. My Kathryn is still an unmarried Miss too, not Mrs, I assured myself. Well now, what about Mrs W. J. Ashburton. George had mentioned that name, Ashburton, had he not? And at least her name could not have been Eleanor! I threw my head back and cackled with both the relief of it and at my own preposterousness. Fancy me imagining that Eleanor – *my* ghost – had been one of the women drowned in the accident and that Kathryn had any connection with the steamer tragedy. At this unseemly outburst (it must be conceded), some of the gentlemen in the Reading Room frowned at me from the other side of the table and whispered to each other. Still, never mind. It must be Winifred or some other female name beginning with a 'W'. Oh, Thank the Lord!

But wait, how could I be so dull? Of course, women cast aside the initials of their Christian names as well as their surnames when they marry... typical! The 'W' and the 'J' would have been her husband's initials! But then, I wonder why they put Kathryn's name in full, and not her husband's initials. Still, newspapers are always crawling with typographical errors. George had said that one of the women's bodies had not been recovered – I wonder which one. Perhaps he will be able to find out from one of the other watermen. I must discover Eleanor's surname somehow – Edward or Kathryn will know it, surely?

But then I suddenly had another terrifying thought. Oh God! On Sunday I had heard the woman on the ghostly ferry scream "William." Oh, God! Oh, God!

I tore the piece from the newspaper, folded it swiftly, and buried it in the pocket of my gown. I dashed out of the Literary Institute, past the small bespectacled man who bawled after me, and up to the house on W____ Hill. Once there I knocked loudly on the freshly cleaned door for the second time that day. It was opened by John, the butler, who upon my enquiry informed me that Kathryn was not at home. Just at that moment Edward approached, dressed in his overcoat and hat,

"Oh, Good Afternoon Jane. Back so soon?"

"Yes," I replied sheepishly, "I would like to see Kathryn this time but I am told she has gone out. Do you know where I might find her?"

"Well, at luncheon today she confessed to me how upset she had been by your visit on Saturday evening and has gone in search of you – she said she was going to try to find you on the Town Pier or in the vicinity. I do not know the details of what went on between the two of you, Jane – and, quite honestly, I do not wish to know. I cannot understand why you have made no effort to come and comfort her since your disagreement. Do you realise it was almost a week ago? I was under the misapprehension that you were her friend. I will see you upon my return Jane, no doubt. Good-day to you."

With that, he slammed the front door behind him and strode away, leaving me standing on the doorstep. I was flabbergasted by his attitude towards me and annoyed that I had not had chance to ask him for Eleanor's surname.

Then, immediately, as panic took hold of me, I knew I must find Kathryn, especially if she were on her way to the Town Pier. I remembered the promise that I had made to George about not going near the river or the pier without him, but I also knew that I must get to Kathryn before Eleanor found her. There was no time to go and hunt for George. Besides, he might be anywhere between here and London.

As I approached the pier I realised with dismay that, yet again, my fears were being realised – I had arrived too late. I could see Eleanor hovering to the right and slightly behind Kathryn at the far end – the part high above the deepest water. Eleanor remained silent just like she had each time I had encountered her and Kathryn did not seem to be aware of her presence. By this time, I was in a state of terror because I was convinced that Eleanor was going to hurt (or do something far worse to) Kathryn, and I still had to reach the end of the pier before I could rescue her. The vision of Eleanor falling headlong into the river on Saturday morning was at the forefront of my mind. Would Eleanor do something as terrible as that to Kathryn? Would she push her over the railings and into the currents? I knew also that, like me, Kathryn was unable to swim. Even if she survived the impact, she would surely drown! I could not let that happen – she is my love, my life.

So, despite my legs feeling as if they were filled with river water, I started running as fast as I could along the pier. Then, suddenly, the opposite of what I was expecting happened! Kathryn turned and lunged towards Eleanor, grappled with her persecutor and flung her from the pier into the icy waters. From where did she derive such strength? A spine-chilling laugh reverberated around the bay. I screamed Kathryn's name, but no sound came from my lips and, seemingly totally unaware of my presence, she darted past me and fled.

Not surprisingly, I was in a state of terrible shock following this uncanny repetition of the one I had witnessed in the early dawn on Saturday, just a few days ago. Well, not quite an exact repetition, I suppose. But the spectre was raised in my mind and I must face it – Kathryn may have caused Eleanor to fall from the pier on the previous occasion too. Had Eleanor been mortal when she had arrived in G____ on Friday night and had Kathryn killed her by pushing her into the river in the darkness of the following dawn? Is that why Eleanor had come back to haunt me – us? Now, here was an even worse menace for me to struggle with – the thought that Kathryn may be a murderer. But why would Kathryn have wanted to kill Eleanor? Surely, there was also the uncertainty that Kathryn was not present – or at least I had not seen her (or anyone else for that matter) – that last time… that last time before daybreak on Saturday morning.

My God, where is Eleanor? Just as before, I threw myself at the rail and searched the icy waters. Just as before, there was no sign of her. Exhausted, I fell, sobbing, to the ground.

William Ashburton

Friday December 21, 1866

After a while I recovered sufficiently to arrive at the hideous realisation that Eleanor had simply vanished and, even worse, I had no idea where Kathryn had gone. Although Kathryn had not been harmed during the confrontation I had just witnessed, I knew that she would be in grave danger if Eleanor pursued her. Indeed, a far more sinister complexion had arisen – I now feared for Kathryn's life. At that moment I could only envisage one eventuality: that Eleanor would succeed in killing Kathryn. Kathryn's life would be over and all hope of us recovering our wonderful life together would be extinguished.

I felt extremely agitated and knew that I must intervene at all costs. In desperation, I rushed to W____ Hill as I assumed Kathryn would have hurried straight home. But she was still missing and no-one had seen her for a number of hours. Indeed, Edward had not returned either. My enquiries clearly caused consternation amongst the servants. I felt terribly alone but the only thing I could do was go home and wait.

Once in my sitting-room I sat down and tried to think clearly, but I was unable to concentrate as my mind was flipping from one sickening vision to another. I would have to pray that George would miraculously be able to stop something atrocious from happening. However, I felt too afraid to walk across the town to make this latest terrible incident known to him. It is such a burden being a useless, weak woman! I tried to read my novel (I was deep into *Lady Audley's Secret*), which I usually found so thrilling, but it only made me more anxious and frightened, and so I had to cease. It saddened me that Kathryn and I were not enjoying it together. Indeed, we were not spending any time together now. Oh, how I missed her in so many ways. I tossed the volume aside and remained staring before me, into empty, desolate space.

Saturday December 22, 1866

The next thing I knew it was morning. I must have slumbered fully dressed on my sitting-room couch as I was awakened by birdsong and a weak ray of sunlight creeping across my eyelids. I was shivering and my neck and limbs felt painfully stiff. Have you ever been awoken on a winter's morning by the beautiful, melodic song of the robin and then immediately had the awful thought slice through your brain that the person you love might be a murderer? No, I do not suppose it is a commonplace affair. For me this recognition was closely followed by another terrible, intrusive realisation – I could not keep this knowledge to myself. I had a duty to make what I had seen known to others, starting with Edward. Betraying the one you love is a terrible, terrible thing – this much I know for sure.

Having thus resolved to break my silence, I hastily changed my attire, attended to my hair and half-ran up to the house on W____ Hill. This time both Edward and Kathryn were present and were sitting at the table when I was shown into the breakfast-room. They both looked startled and, as I was to discover, not simply because of my unexpected entrance. Upon seeing Kathryn, I went to her and said soothingly,

"My Darling, thank goodness you are safe."

I opened my arms to embrace her, but she shrank from me and I was left standing beside her not knowing what to do. I felt hurt by her rejection but as I studied her I was astounded by how pale and thin she looked. It was as though she had not slept nor eaten since I had visited her at home, exactly a week ago.

Feeling desperate, I pleaded with them both to tell me the truth... the entire story.

After a long silence, during which they looked at each other and my expectations were raised that I would finally be brought in from the cold, Kathryn said... and oh... in such an icy tone,

"Please leave, Jane... there is nothing you can do to help. You are interfering and, by doing so, you are making the situation far, far worse."

As she said this she glared at me long and hard as though she hated me and then she stood up and left the room. Yes, she actually left the room!

As the door closed I turned my attention to Edward and told him of the terrible trials I had suffered during the past week. When I had finished relating the shocking scene in which Kathryn had caused Eleanor to plummet from the pier, he dropped his face into his hands and let out a long, low groan,

"Oh, Jane. Yes, alright, I shall tell you all I know, but I fear there is still much that I am ignorant of."

"Yes, Edward, you must. The time has come."

"But first, I beg of you, do not divulge any of this to the Police until I can give you my assurance that it is safe to do so – please, for Kathryn's sake."

My unwavering love for Kathryn made this an easy promise to make.

Having received my pledge, Edward continued,

"Kathryn and I have grown up with the understanding that our paternal grandmother, also called Kathryn Lawton, was killed in that very accident on the *Margery*. By the way, Kathryn is said to bear a striking resemblance to her. There have also been extremely disturbing rumours that our grandmother was murdered, but our family has never discovered what happened. Such secrets amongst loved ones are insidious and Kathryn and I share strong feelings about our grandfather Lawton, and indeed our mother, having gone to their graves without knowing the truth. As you know our father is ill and growing weaker by the day and his last remaining wish is that we find out what happened to his mother when he was a young boy.

"Consequently, and I confess I did not tell you the full story last year, our primary reason for moving to G____ was to find out what really took place on that fateful night in 1815. But before we left London this Eleanor woman materialised and started haunting, literally haunting, Kathryn. I do not know who she is. As you are aware, she has followed us here and I know

Kathryn is keeping things from me. Furthermore, I felt that if she had wanted you to know more then she would have told you. I have noticed that she has been distant towards you since Eleanor arrived in G____, Jane, but I believe this has been because she has wanted to keep you and Eleanor apart – to protect you from her, I mean.

"This morning at breakfast Kathryn told me that Eleanor's name is Ashburton and I assume she is a relative of Mrs W. J. Ashburton, the other woman who drowned in 1815. Incidentally, none of our remaining family were acquainted with Mrs W. J. Ashburton and I presume that she and our grandmother were strangers too. Although, obviously, we cannot be sure of that. If there were a connection between them, we do not know what it was. I expect that, like us, Eleanor simply wants to find out what happened.

"I do not believe she is a ghost, Jane. I do not believe in ghosts. What sane person does? Surely *you* do not think…"

"Yes, I do believe Eleanor is a ghost, Edward," I said and sank into a chair, suddenly terribly wearied as a consequence of speaking the words aloud, "How else can we explain the happenings that I have experienced latterly?"

Edward gave me a penetrating look before replying,

"Well, you yourself have said that at times you are unsure whether you can trust the veracity of your mind and that you may have been hallucinating. From my own experience I know that the female mind can sometimes be nervous – weak even…"

"Please... please Edward, do not say that. I too fear at times that I have lost the balance of my mind. Who would not think that in the circumstances?"

"Yes indeed, but consider the unbalancing effect of those ridiculous sensation novels Kathryn has told me you are reading compulsively – *The Woman in Something*, *Lady Somebody's Secret* – am I right?"

"What of it?"

"Oh Jane, must I really explain?"

"Hush Edward, there is something else I need to tell you. I have heard that the body of one woman was never recovered."

"Well Jane, it could not have been Grandmother Lawton because I can assure you that we buried her in the family vault. It was terrible... terrible."

"Yes, you must have buried someone. Are you certain it was her? A body that has been submerged in river water for some time would be unrecognisable."

"Jane, for Heaven's sake. You are being disgusting and preposterous! I cannot believe you are suggesting... no, I am sorry, but no."

"Well I... but wait Edward, I have an idea. There may be a way in which we can find out further details about the tragedy and, more importantly, discover who Eleanor was and what happened to her."

"But Jane... this is ludicrous!"

"Listen to me. You have just confirmed what I read yesterday in last year's newspaper – that the other woman who drowned was officially named as Mrs W. J. Ashburton. We do not yet know for sure whether her Christian name was Eleanor because we only have her husband's initials. Surely, there is a possibility that W. J. Ashburton Esquire is still alive? He would be exceedingly old – in his seventies, perhaps – but it is not impossible is it?"

"Well, yes, I suppose he could be. But I do not really see what Eleanor has to do with the accident all those years ago…"

"Oh, Edward! It may be my woman's intuition and I may be wrong, but I am terrified that the tragedy will be repeated in some dreadful way on the anniversary… on Christmas Eve. Only this time it would be Kathryn…"

"Kathryn! What are you saying, Jane? You do not mean to suggest that someone plans to murder Kathryn!" he exclaimed.

I continued urgently, aware that I was staring at him with eyes that were wide with terror,

"No, not someone, Edward, I mean Eleanor… can you not see – after what I witnessed yesterday? Oh God, Christmas Eve is on Monday – the day after tomorrow! We must hurry. If Mr Ashburton is alive then surely we could find him and implore him to help us work out how to break free of Eleanor – to get Kathryn free of her. We must be rid of her. Do you think you could use your contacts to find out if he is still alive? If he is, we need his address and then I shall write to him. Also, I suspect that his first name may be William. We have that to go on, at least."

"Yes, yes, of course. We must act, yes and quickly too, if… if, as you suppose, Kathryn's life is in danger. I am not at all convinced but I cannot take the risk… Oh God, the very thought… it would be too awful."

There was not a moment to lose. While Edward set off on his quest, I waited impatiently in the breakfast-room, unable to settle to anything, while the servants cleared away the remains of the breakfast that had barely been touched. Finally, just as I could hear the appetising clinking of cutlery in preparation for luncheon in the nearby dining-room, Edward reappeared looking grimly pleased with himself and brandishing a piece of paper in his hand. He placed it in front of me on the table and I read the name, William James Ashburton Esquire, followed by the address of Boar's, a gentleman's club in St. James's, London. At the bottom someone had scribbled that, apparently, Mr Ashburton could be found taking lunch there on most days of the week.

I kissed Edward on the cheek, agreed to his demand that I show him the letter before I sent it, went home and composed it as speedily as I could.

**

At this point Dr Westcott laid Jane Waterford's manuscript aside and took up another document consisting of a couple of hand-written pages, from which he carried on:

Letter from Miss Jane Waterford to William J. Ashburton Esquire, dated December 22, 1866.

Dear Mr Ashburton

As I am sure you will appreciate, by the time you have read to the conclusion of this letter, it has been an extremely trying one for me to compose. Please also accept my sincere apologies for raising the subject that I am about to speak of. I hope it does not cause you too great a degree of distress.

I have it on good authority that one of the women, who tragically drowned as a result of falling overboard from the ferryboat, the Margery, *on Christmas Eve 1815 soon after it left the Town Pier in my home town of G___, was your wife. I also understand that she was one of two women who lost their lives that night in the accident; the other being a Mrs Kathryn Lawton, also a resident of Chelsea. I do not know for certain that the two women were acquainted, but I suspect they were.*

I have been unable to discover your wife's Christian name from the newspaper report of the calamity, but I am writing to you to let you know that an elderly woman, named Eleanor Ashburton, has recently materialised in G___. Moreover, she appears to have more than a passing interest in the tragedy. Is she a relative of yours and/or related to your late wife?

Alternatively, could it be possible that she is the ghost of your late wife? I do not want to put too much of what I have endured during the last week in writing. However, this being has powers that are not wholly human but are – yes, I have to say it – this being has powers that I can only describe as unearthly.

I have become acquainted with a brother and sister, Edward Lawton Esquire and Miss Kathryn Lawton who are the grandchildren of the late Mrs Kathryn Lawton. They have recently moved to G____ in order to discover the truth of what occurred that fateful night. However, Eleanor Ashburton is inhibiting the progress of their enquiries by haunting, yes literally haunting, Kathryn to the extent that I am afraid for her life. Conversely, Eleanor Ashburton seems to have no interest in Edward whatsoever.

Equally disturbing is the knowledge that I have unearthed from the local men who currently work on the steamboat ferries. I have discovered that the body of one of the women was never recovered, although I do not know which one.

I am sorry to be writing to you in this manner and I would not be doing so if I did not believe it to be a matter of life and death. I would be eternally grateful to you if you could reply by return to firstly reassure me that your wife's Christian name was not Eleanor. Having done so, please let me know if you have any idea of the identity of this apparition, and inform me of any knowledge you have regarding which of the two women's bodies was not found. Finally, it goes without saying that Edward Lawton and I appeal for your assistance in ensuring the banishment of Eleanor Ashburton from G____ before the anniversary of the tragedy on Christmas Eve.

Although I usually reside in G____, I have taken a room in a lodging house on Margery Street,

*Clerkenwell and ask you to send your reply to the
address at the top of this letter.*

Returning to the manuscript, Dr Westcott
continued reading.

Having written the most difficult letter that I
have ever had the misfortune to write in my lifetime, I
decided that I could not countenance the delay that
would be caused by returning to Edward and arguing
over its finer points and its mode of delivery. I knew
that he would insist on taking it himself. Also, he
would not have allowed me to send a letter that
associated the Lawton name with the spectral sphere;
nor one that made reference to the rumour about a
missing corpse.

Besides, the work had already taken far longer
than I had wished as I had resolved to make a copy of
the letter for my own keeping. Rather, in my agitation,
I determined that I would deliver it in person to
William James Ashburton Esquire at Boar's. I
supposed that he would linger at the club after
consuming a full luncheon.

As I write this now I can appreciate with
hindsight that this decision was a terrible error.

I packed my overnight *portmanteau*, sent a
note to Edward telling him of my intentions, and
narrowly caught the afternoon ferry to London. My
heart sank when I saw that, inevitably, it was the
Margery but, once we were underway, I espied George
and the sight of him engendered a growing feeling in
me that all would be well. Although it was cold I

decided to stay outside on the deck as I did not want to be cooped up below in the saloon with all the other passengers on the crowded boat. I was in no mood for unwanted attention.

At first I was gazing absent-mindedly at the bank rushing by, while the river became increasingly narrow and claustrophobic. As I became deep in thought I happened to look over the side of the ferry and down into the depths of the water and, for a while, the effect was mesmerising and somewhat comforting. But, what I saw next has been the subject of the nightmare that I have suffered each time I have slept since that terrible day.

It was a body – a woman's naked and decomposing body – floating just below the surface of the water amongst the reeking detritus. Horror of horrors, it was keeping alongside the boat! I could not recognise it because it had been submerged long enough for it to have become swollen and discoloured. But I knew. Even more disgusting, certain soft parts of her face – the eyes, the nose – had disintegrated. They appeared simply as hollows, as black as the pupils that must have once inhabited the eye-sockets, in awful contrast to the pale green of her skin. Unbelievably, the anaemic lips were still present and she was… she was sneering at me triumphantly.

Suddenly, her lips parted, revealing long yellow teeth like the tusks of a walrus. I felt as though I had no breath – as though I were drowning, but somehow I managed to scream and scream and scream. Men came running. I remember seeing George. They stopped the boat. We turned back. A search was made. But nothing... nothing... no body... nobody was found. I felt sure, at that moment, that I had lost my mind.

Such a shock was enough to make me resolve to give up, to go home and hide. Indeed, when I informed George of all that had occurred since we had last met, he advised me to leave the letter with him and he would take it. But no, I felt I would be letting Kathryn down if I failed to deliver it and wait for the response myself. A reply arriving by the postal service would be too late. I had to do everything within, and beyond, my own powers.

Once settled in my room in the lodging house, I ordered a hansom cab to take me directly to Boar's. It was a tiresome journey and one that left me greatly in need of refreshment. However, as a woman I was, of course, barred from entering the club and so, having deposited the letter with the steward, I left. As I did so, I felt certain that I was being scrutinised from one of the many windows that constituted that exclusive institution.

Sunday December 23, 1866

Early the next morning Mrs Breddon, the lodging house owner, slipped a chilling reply from William Ashburton under my door, which I read with trembling hands.

***

Once again Dr Westcott laid Jane Waterford's manuscript aside and picked up a second, shorter hand-written letter, from which he carried on:

Letter from William J. Ashburton Esquire to Miss Jane Waterford, dated December 23, 1866.

Dear Miss Waterford

I am sure you will not be surprised to learn that I was repulsed by your offensive letter concerning my dear late wife, Eleanor. Yes, her Christian name was Eleanor, but I assure you that nothing of which you write can be inferred from that simple fact.

I am totally at a loss to know who this mortal woman – yes, I do mean mortal woman – could be, as neither I nor my first wife have a single surviving relative. I can only conclude that this entire story is impossible. Indeed, it is nothing but a complete fabrication invented by yourself.

Likewise, I know nothing concerning the missing corpse and can only suggest that your ferrymen are spreading malicious gossip that has no foundation in truth. The remains of my wife are interred in the cemetery of Saint George's Church in G____, as you can verify for yourself should you wish to do so.

I do believe you are out of your mind. If you contact me again I shall take steps to have you certified and locked away in a lunatic asylum. Conveniently for me, I am in possession of your letter as evidence of your insanity. Do not doubt my

*determination as I have already succeeded in
disposing of my second and third wives in like manner.
I trust this will be the end of the matter.*

Again, Dr Westcott carefully laid the letter
down and continued reading from the manuscript.

As soon as I had finished reading the letter,
still shaking, I packed my bag, settled my account with
Mrs Breddon and fled back to G____.

Christmas Eve 1866

Monday December 24, 1866

All of a sudden Christmas Eve was upon us. My God, was it only yesterday? The passing of time has lost all meaning. It was the day that I had been dreading since my conversation with George in the schoolroom. I usually loved Christmas and everything associated with it. Last year Kathryn and I had spent this special date together at the house in W____ Hill, wrapping gifts, decorating the tree and supervising the preparations within the household for the Yuletide festivities. Edward had been in residence too and in a celebratory mood, although he kept us under tight surveillance. Even so, it had been wonderful.

Oh, but this year, my feelings could not have been more at odds, more in contrast, to my recollection of that former occasion. I was separated from Kathryn and I felt utterly inconsolable. Yes, the prospect of the day provoked feelings in me which were more akin to the years immediately following my father's death, before Kathryn and I met, but they were worse, much, much worse. A part of me – a cruel aspect – hoped Kathryn felt the same.

I was puzzled that Edward had not attempted to contact me – about William Ashburton and the letter, I mean. At the time, I assumed he had remained at home to comfort Kathryn and attempt to raise her spirits.

Since conversing with George last Thursday evening I had been convinced that my encounter with the ghostly ferry had been a forewarning and that Kathryn's life was in danger. Understandably, I now believed that Eleanor represented the most likely source of threat. Indeed, I was certain that the tragedy of Christmas Eve 1815 would be repeated in some form, unless I took drastic action to prevent it. Therefore, as early in the morning as I could manage, I positioned myself at the far end of the Town Pier, high above the churning waters, and examined the phizzog of every person who embarked on each ferry bound for London. I reasoned that, only by doing so could I make sure that Eleanor did not succeed in escaping from my sight, nor in spiriting my beloved Kathryn away with her – of luring her to her death. Even having reassured myself that they were not on board, as each steamer set off from the Town Pier my senses were heightened as I watched and listened intently, expecting something dreadful to happen. However, nothing occurred – at least, not during daylight hours.

As darkness fell, dense fog enfolded the pier causing the usually bright lamps to be made hazy by dancing beads of water. Christmas Eve had arrived and it was nearing the hour when the last ferry was due to depart. It was already moored alongside the pier awaiting its London-bound passengers. In horror, but also with a certain morbid sense of inevitability, I read the name on its side: the *Margery*.

Worse was to come.

By this point, both my body and my mind were numb with exhaustion and the cold, and it took many seconds for me to register that I was staring at the forms of Kathryn and Eleanor hurrying along the pier towards me. Indeed, they were already close. Both wore travelling-cloaks of black velvet with the hoods around their heads against the moisture and, as a consequence, they had seemed to materialise out of the gloom. I watched in horror as they approached and went straight past me, as if I too were a spectre. But, like them, I had covered my head and part of my face with my hood and that, combined with the murkiness, resulted in neither of them appearing to notice my presence. Indeed, in addition, the attention of each figure was focussed intently on the waiting ferryboat. While they had passed, I had realised that, although they appeared to the casual onlooker to be walking arm-in-arm, Eleanor was actually forcing Kathryn along. Before I could react, they had embarked onto the steamer and Eleanor was blocking Kathryn's escape to dry land.

I was now even more persuaded that the tragedy was going to be re-enacted.

All at once I heard Edward calling my name. I turned to see him running along the pier. But it was too late. The ferry was departing. I could not let it leave without me. So, despite not having a ticket, I dashed down the ladder to the boat just as it was starting to be pulled in. I nearly dropped into the tossing waters and this desperate act caused more of a commotion than I would have liked in the circumstances. Just as I was fearing that I would be evicted, George came forward to vouch for me and I was allowed to remain. While the ferry moved away, I could see Edward doubled up on the pier, fighting for breath, as helpless as a woman.

I later discovered that, when Edward had received my note and realised that I was not planning to discuss the letter with him before delivering it, he had determined to travel to London himself to speak to Mr Ashburton at Boar's, rationally and gentleman-to-gentleman. That was why I had not heard from him. However, by the time Edward had arrived, William Ashburton was nowhere to be seen. Thus, Edward, like myself, had achieved nothing.

Worse still, in going he had left Kathryn unprotected.

It is up to you, Dr Westcott, to judge whether or not I took the best course of action by boarding the ferry that night. It is clear to me now that sometimes we have an exaggerated notion of the extent to which we can alter the course of events or the fate of those we love. In that moment I did what I thought was right and I will never know whether, had I taken a different path, the outcome would have been better or worse.

No, it could not have been more disastrous. Indeed, I can hardly bring myself to carry on. The ensuing events are almost too terrible to relate. But of course, I must continue.

The ferryboat was crowded and it took me considerable time to find Eleanor and Kathryn, but I did discover them just as we had gathered speed and entered deep waters. All the other passengers had settled themselves comfortably in the warmth of the dining saloon below but, despite the freezing temperature, the two hooded figures stood at the stern, on the deserted deck. Eleanor was no longer clutching Kathryn's arm. I heard faint laughter – that same menacing sound. I could barely think due to the steamer's overwhelming noise and vibration. Perhaps the clinging had just been for show, simply an act for my sake, to make it seem as though Kathryn did not really want to leave G____. I did not know what to think anymore nor whom I might trust. I could hardly believe that I had lost my faith in Kathryn, after everything we had gone through together. It was a living nightmare. Perhaps she was leaving G____ perfectly willingly, after all. Perhaps she had capitulated because she wanted to return to London in order to start a new life – a married life – away from Edward and her father. And... I thought in desperation... away from me.

That spectre had always haunted our love.

As I write this, it is hard for me to determine the exact sequence of events as they all took place so quickly. I remember hearing a gentleman's voice behind me,

"Jane... Miss Jane Waterford? What a lovely surprise! But what are you doing on this ferry, this night of all nights?"

I turned to see Mr Knight, an old friend of my late father, who had recognised me and who, it later transpired, was concerned for my welfare having witnessed the rumpus surrounding my arrival onto the boat. Before I could answer him, my nightmare worsened. While my attention was focussed on Mr Knight, I saw his face register alarm from something that was happening behind me. By the time I turned back to where Kathryn and Eleanor had been standing, they had both vanished. In panic we rushed to the stern together and, peering over, saw both women falling down, down, towards the deep, dark, icy waters. I watched in horror as Kathryn struck the churning, foaming waters and in an instant we left her behind. I shall never forget that terrible sight and the dreadful thud of the impact. I heard two women screaming and screaming and screaming – one was Kathryn and the other... was me.

My confusion was great as the paddle-wheels of the steamboat were making a deafening cacophony. So, I did not realise at the time, but it dawned on me later, that I had heard no sound when Eleanor entered the water, nor did she scream. Nonetheless, I am absolutely certain that she fell and that, despite the fog and the dark, I saw her plunge into the water. It had been the same when she had plummeted from the pier. There are no mortal women who do not scream in such terrible circumstances. I remember Mr Knight thundered 'Man Overboard!' and exhorted the captain to turn the boat around, to retrace its path to the position from where the women had disappeared.

This he did but, of course, it took time – and it seemed interminable. When we reached that awful place, George and another waterman hurled themselves into the river. Life-buoys were flung after them. Men were shouting in desperation. Kathryn was still visible in the bright lights given off by the ferry. I do not know what was happening to Eleanor because my eyes were fixed on Kathryn who was repeatedly disappearing and resurfacing, and still screaming. George, for my sake I am sure, determined to try to save her rather than Eleanor. But, as I watched, something inexplicable happened. Just as he was about to clasp her, he abandoned his attempt and, instead, helped his fellow crew member bring Eleanor back to the boat so that the others were able to haul her back on board. I screamed at George but by the time he returned to the water to try to rescue Kathryn for the second time, she had vanished. Almost immediately a doctor, who had been travelling as a passenger, pronounced that Eleanor was dead. George had rescued her for nothing as far as I was concerned and, in so doing, had let Kathryn drown.

I clung to Mr Knight, sobbing and sobbing, as I tried to take in the awful fact that Kathryn was gone.

She had left me forever.

Bawley Bay

Monday December 24, 1866 (late evening)

After the search for Kathryn was abandoned, the *Margery* had returned to the Town Pier and a shrouded body had been carried from the ferry and was lying on the pier under George's watchful eye. The vessel set off for London once more but I too remained as I had no purpose in travelling there. I felt utterly forlorn.

As it was Christmas Eve, Mr Knight needed to return to his family, although he had reluctantly stayed on the ferry. Before we parted he told me that, with my permission, he would call on me when the festivities were over, to check that I had recovered. Indeed, he attempted to persuade me to accompany him to the capital and spend the day with his relations, but I declined as, I am sure you can imagine, I was in no mood for celebration. I assured him that I would be staying with friends, but acquiesced to his proposed visit after Christmas.

So, Mr Knight instructed me to go home, saying that he would deal with the Police enquiries. Police enquiries! The phrase shook me to the core of my being. I wonder whether he saw it written on my face. If he did he must have assumed that I was traumatised, having witnessed such a terrible scene. Of course, as a woman, it would have been inappropriate for me to ask him what precisely he had seen on the deck that had shocked him so much, especially as he had no idea of my connection with the drowned ladies. I am sorry to confess that I did not let him into my confidence.

After watching the ferryboat recede from view, I traipsed back along the pier to the High Street and blundered along the river bank until I reached the glutinous silt of Bawley Bay. If anyone is lost in the River Thames at G____, and their bloated corpse is found by the men who seek out such vile things, they are always brought to Bawley Bay... eventually. That is the place to wait. That is where I needed to wait for Kathryn.

While I had edged past the shrouded body, George had been standing beside it with his head bowed but, so soon after the tragedy, I had not been able to address him. I needed an explanation concerning why he had given up his attempt to save Kathryn, but I could not cope with hearing it yet.

As I stumbled to the far side of the bay and looked back towards the town, I realised that the fog had lifted and the moon was shining brightly. Consequently, it was possible to see far into the distance, even on the river, although it was a creepy effect, utterly unlike daylight. Everything was clothed in shades of black, grey and silver. All was silent.

After many hours, as I watched cautiously, I suddenly caught sight of an approaching rowing boat and Mr Dickens' words from *Our Mutual Friend* that Kathryn and I had read together, hammered into my brain,

What he had in tow, lunged itself at him sometimes in an awful manner when the boat was checked, and sometimes seemed to try to wrench itself away, though for the most part it followed submissively.

When we recited them, I could never have imagined how pertinent they would become in this horrible, horrible manner.

The waterman heaved the boat onto the shore and others helped him carry Kathryn's body on a makeshift stretcher and lay her down carefully amongst the bawley boats on the exposed sand-bank of our beloved River Thames. After resting a while they lifted her gently and took her within the Waterside Mission building, so that she was sheltered from the bitterly cold wind. Their protective tending of her belied the truth of what I knew for certain. She was dead – drowned. She could not have possibly survived. I wept as I remembered that I could no longer have any claim on her in life, whilst I was tormented by the fear of who had claimed her now that she was dead. After a while Edward arrived and, from my vantage point, I saw him enter the Mission. The fact that he did not soon re-appear told me all I needed to know.

By this time a small crowd was gathering near the entrance to the Mission building, despite the late hour. Some townspeople stared and nodded in my direction – I could tell that they were speaking about me. I wanted to melt into the air. I knew that I must prevent them from penetrating my emotions. I must not let my facial expression divulge the feelings for Kathryn that I had kept locked away in a labyrinthine web of secrets – for the sake of her memory. Kathryn and I had laboured hard to keep our passion buried in the deepest darkness, like an infinite galaxy without stars. In time, precious things cease to thrive if they are deprived of light and, I think, this is what happened to our love. However, this is only a small part of the story, and my life has been without joy, since Eleanor arrived.

I turned away from the dull, rolling, mud-coloured waters in haste because I felt compelled to lunge into the river's icy depths, so that I too could lie senseless on the shore. I wanted to lie by Kathryn's side once more, and be with her forever. But I knew that someone else was already there; *Eleanor* was already there.

Despite my feelings of anger towards George I remember wishing he were here so that I could question him. I needed to know what had prevented him from rescuing Kathryn… from saving her life. George was not here, nor did I imagine that Edward would want me to join him at Kathryn's side in so public a setting. Therefore, I decided to go home. Although I reckoned that the Police might have contacted William Ashburton by now, to inform him of Eleanor's fate, I resolved to write to him again because I refused to accept that he had no connection with this dreadful apparition. I recognised that he would find this letter even more provocative than the previous one and it would generate an angrier response from him. I loathed the thought of commencing such a task.

But before I could leave, I heard George calling my name. He startled me by placing his hands on my shoulders and looking directly into my eyes. Rushing his words, he said,

"She's gone Miss, she's gone. I lifted the shroud and it's not her – it's someone else I've never even seen before. Oh God, Miss, she's got the better of us! She's got the better of us!"

Before I could ask him what he meant, he carried on,

"I've spoken to the watermen just back from London on the *Margery* and they say she's the same woman I rescued, but I don't believe it, Miss. I don't recognise her.

"Oh Miss, I tried to save Miss Lawton, I really did, with all my strength, but when I got close it was like an invisible force was at work, preventing me from getting hold of her. I'm so sorry, Miss. I'm so sorry. I know... I know how terrible it feels to lose someone you love."

At this point I interrupted and implored him to explain who was gone.

He again blurted his words out,

"It's Mrs Ashburton, Miss – I don't... I don't know what else to call her. You saw a corpse lying on the pier under a shroud earlier, but it's not her, Miss. It's not the body I rescued from the water, it's another woman, but she's a stranger – I've never set eyes on her before. I thought we had her, Miss, but Mrs Ashburton's plain vanished."

I felt a chill of horror. It could not be that yet another woman had suffered a grisly death in this catastrophe. Worse still, Eleanor was still at large.

"No George, you must be mistaken. Tell me it is not true," I said hoarsely. My throat felt horribly constricted.

"No, 'tis true, Miss, you saw me pull her from the water. She felt heavy, just like a mortal being. The crew hauled her onto the boat and we placed her on the Town Pier when we arrived back in G____. The doctor too, on the steamer... he was taken in... he thought she was human... he said she was dead, but she's vanished now, simply vanished."

"Oh George, will we never be free of this?"

"I don't know Miss. Also, it all happened just like we feared it would. I saw Mrs Ashburton push Miss Lawton over the side of the ferry. Mrs Ashburton then went in after her, of her own accord like."

Yes, one or both of them must have gone over voluntarily, unless somebody else had been there and pushed them both over, but I had seen no-one.

"Are you absolutely sure that you did not see anyone else George? Did you not see someone near them who could have pushed them over?"

"No Miss, I saw you on deck talking to your gentleman friend, but there was nobody else. Oh God, Miss, I'd thought this was going to be the end of it. I thought we had her."

George and I looked at each other with wide-eyed horror and then he started running towards the Waterside Mission building to deliver his awful news.

I doubted that anyone would believe him. For my part, I had witnessed enough. I could not take any more and needed to get away. I was in a state of near collapse; my body was leaden and my head felt as if it had been clouted with an oar. Laboriously, I made my way away from the river to seek the relative sanctuary of home. Once there I would begin my grim task of writing to William Ashburton for the second time. I needed him to tell me the truth about Eleanor. I knew that if I gave him a full account of this evening's events, as I intended to do, he would most certainly carry out his threat of having me placed in an asylum. But after what George had just told me, in addition to everything else that had transpired, what choice did I have?

The Cemetery at Saint George's

Monday December 24, 1866 (nearing midnight)

Even with hindsight I do not know why I avoided going directly home as I had intended, nor why I was drawn to visit the cemetery in Saint George's Churchyard instead. While I trudged along the empty streets I started to plan my letter to William Ashburton and perhaps that was what reminded me of his written assurance that Eleanor's remains were interred there. I suspected that his expression of endearment for her in his letter had been disingenuous. How else could I interpret his having buried her in G____ rather than have her returned to be near him in London?

But what about the speculation that one of the women's bodies had never been found? This he had vehemently denied. Most rumours have some foundation in truth and this one had been passed down among the watermen from generation to generation – does that not suggest it must have veracity? Moreover, George had just told me that the drowned body in Eleanor's form that he had pulled from the river had vanished. Even more inexplicably, the shrouded woman who had replaced her had transpired to be someone unknown to us. I had terrible feelings of hatred towards this man. Surely he could have prevented tonight's tragic events, if only he had taken some action.

I was absorbed in these grim thoughts when I reached the cemetery. By this time the night had become murkier as the moon was obscured by cloud. As a consequence, I had trouble deciphering the memorials chiselled on the various gravestones. I was about to abandon my task, thinking that it would make more sense to return in daylight, when the silver orb unexpectedly reappeared and the illumination revealed an old man standing in front of one of the graves on the opposite side of the graveyard. Although initially this was a fearful shock, I decided that I could not give way to cowardice at this late stage and so I started moving hesitantly towards him. My body felt stiff with fear. Despite the fact that he was facing the tombstone and did not turn to look at me as I approached, I had a sense that he was expecting me, and that he had been waiting for some time.

When I had almost reached him I spoke, although my voice sounded peculiar, even to me,

"Mr William Ashburton?" I asked.

"Yes, I am William Ashburton, and I assume you, Madam, are Miss Jane Waterford," he replied coldly as he turned to face me.

I nodded and for a while we stood contemplating each other in silence. I do not know what he thought of me in my disarray, but I saw a man who seemed to be under an enormous degree of strain. By the light of the moon, I could see that his hair was pure white, his face deeply lined, and his eyes bulging and bloodshot. After a while I turned away from him to read the words on the headstone and received confirmation that it belonged to Eleanor Ashburton and that her date of death was 24th December 1815. He was the first to speak,

"It is time for the truth to be told and I can confess it to you as no-one will rely on your testimony should you relate it to others. No, no-one will believe the story of a madwoman, a Crazy Jane, who claims to see people on the other side."

I said nothing despite his insulting words, but waited impatiently for him to continue.

"When my wife, Eleanor, and I had been married for two years I began to have suspicions that she was being unfaithful. I am a patient body, Miss Waterford, and so I followed her until eventually, one day, I discovered her in an amorous embrace, not with a gentleman as I had suspected, but with another female. They were kissing each other passionately (not that that means anything between women), but I could not ignore it either. Indeed, her 'friend' was also a married woman. *Her* name was Kathryn Lawton – the grandmother of your precious Kathryn. Your precious, dead, Kathryn.

"When I questioned Eleanor she responded with the utmost cruelty. She told me that she did not love me, had never loved me, but had only married me so that she could avoid living a life of poverty. You see, Miss Waterford, in those days, it was inconceivable that a woman of her class would work and so her only option was to marry and be financially supported by a gentleman. It was my misfortune that she had chosen me for this convenience.

"Of course, I did not take any of it seriously and I wanted us to stay together. I mean, after all, what could they possibly do together without a man? I wanted her to end the alliance and for us to resume our marriage as if nothing had happened. I was even prepared for her to continue with her attachment as long as she remained with me. I still loved her, you see, Miss Waterford."

He broke down and sobbed quietly until he was able to resume, which he did with greater vitriol,

"However, when she refused to end her pitiful friendship, or to stay with me, I knew that I had to do something. A few days later I discovered that they were planning a cosy Christmas Eve visit to your miserable town's pleasure gardens on one of the new-fangled steamboat ferries. I shadowed them all day waiting for my opportunity but, unfortunately, as their departure time approached, she noticed me. She suddenly espied me as she reached the end of the pier and was about to board the last ferry of the evening – the wretched *Margery*. Forced to act, I ran up to her and attempted to push her from the pier, and I very nearly succeeded, but that Kathryn woman was strong and heaved her back. Before I knew it they had both escaped onto the ferry."

I gasped. So, when I encountered Eleanor on the pier before daybreak just over a week ago, it was William that she had suddenly caught sight of over my shoulder and been transfixed by; and it was him with whom I had watched her grappling. Just as he said, I had seen her fall, but not enter the water. Not William as he is now, but William as he would have been in 1815, young and strong and… intent… on murder!

He continued,

"I did not join the ferry until the last moment and so she was ignorant of the fact that I was also on board... yes... yes, I was also on board. Yes, I was there."

He paused seemingly lost in thought, and then resumed,

"Watching them laughing together, at the stern, made me violently angry – I suspected they were mocking me and I lost control. At least, my rage gave me the courage to do what I had planned to do all along. Of course, I was a young man then and so it was surprisingly easy to push them both over. By the time somebody raised the alarm and the ferry returned to where they had entered the water, there was no sign of them.

"Yes, I lied to you in my letter about something else too – Kathryn Lawton's body was never found. This is why my Eleanor is destined to be seeking her... in the river... forever."

So, it *was* Grandmother Lawton! The family must have interred the wrong person. Oh no, how awful. It is poor consolation, but thank goodness Kathryn has been spared this revelation.

"So now you know the truth, Miss Waterford. I killed them both. Eleanor really is buried here – I did not lie about that – but every day since Christmas Eve 1815, my wife's apparition has haunted me morning, noon and night, and made my life a misery. As you see, my spirit is broken but, even so, I have no intention of being tried for murder after all these years, nor of facing the terrible punishment that would be meted out to me."

I had listened to everything in silence because I was struck dumb in horror at hearing that not only was William Ashburton a double murderer (and of course I was standing alone with him in a deserted graveyard in the dead of night), but also that his words had provided the conclusive evidence that Eleanor Ashburton was indeed the ghost of a woman who had died in the 1815 tragedy. Clearly, there was no reason to suppose that her apparition would stop tormenting me. What a terrible, terrible vision!

I gasped again. To my mind, Eleanor, or at least her restless ghost, was not merely continually searching for Kathryn's grandmother, but she had also been imprisoned in a continual repetition of her own and her lover's murder – at William Ashburton's hand. How truly awful!

Yes, I was facing an abysmal prospect indeed. Eleanor's ghost had caused further loss of life this evening – she had murdered the shrouded woman; she had murdered my Kathryn and taken her as her own, in place of Kathryn's grandmother. Edward had said that they were of similar appearance. She must have been waiting for my Kathryn all these years. Each replaying of the tragedy that I and the watermen had heard was a horrific premonition, culminating in this evening's catastrophe. That is why we had only ever heard one body – Kathryn's – enter the water. That is why I only heard a single body enter the water tonight. Oh, Kathryn, Kathryn!

Presumably tonight's deed had also been a form of Eleanor's revenge on William, as it might prompt the Police to investigate the accident, or murder, as I now knew it to be, of 1815 again. But it was also directed at me, to stop me having the life she had wanted but had had taken away. Well, she had achieved that. I gulped back the tears as I remembered that there was no doubt of that. She had both Kathryns now.

I could not imagine that my situation could worsen and yet William Ashburton had not finished,

"So, Miss Waterford, although I am old, I am not too feeble to have you put away in an asylum. I have an excellent understanding with Dr Westcott, the medical superintendent at the City of London Lunatic Asylum. He will do what I instruct him without asking too many questions. I will reward him of course, but he will be more than willing because, like me, he believes that the world needs to rid itself of unnatural freaks like you. Also, as far as this evening's events are concerned, I am sure the Police will conclude that *you* pushed Miss Kathryn Lawton and her companion overboard in a fit of jealousy, and... of course, I know you are aware by now that it is not Eleanor's body lying on the Town Pier, but a poor woman who has never done you any harm. Oh yes... my wife is very clever."

"I have witnesses who can vouch for my innocence – Mr Knight and George Coombes!" I interrupted, panic-stricken at this unexpected turn of events.

"Unfortunately, your Mr Knight met with an accident as he walked home along the riverbank following his disembarkation from the ferry at London Bridge. It could not be helped. It is easy to trip on an uneven path in the dark and fall into the filthy, coursing river at high tide. No-one could be expected to survive such a mishap."

"Oh God, no," I sobbed, but then gathering myself, I cried, "But I have just spoken to George and he is adamant he saw Eleanor push Kathryn over the side and that she then went over herself. I know George will bear witness and protect me."

"Well, yes, but who is going to be swayed by a story like that? What would be the explanation or the motive? For that matter, even the ferrymen are saying that George Coombes has gone mad because of the stress of tonight's exploits, especially coming so soon after the death of his babe. Apparently he is talking of supernatural forces stopping him rescuing Miss Lawton, and of the dead woman changing her identity. Hah!

"Oh no, Miss Waterford, the Police are much more likely to attribute the murders to you, with jealousy as the primary motive. Witnesses will have seen you standing like an agitated wraith on the pier all day, scrutinising the faces of all who passed you, until the ones you were interested in appeared. Indeed, many of the crew and ferry passengers noticed your clumsy and desperate arrival on the ferry in pursuit of the two women. Furthermore, no-one will believe the words of your ignorant, insane ferryman over and above a gentleman of my standing any more than they will trust a madwoman like you. I shall leave now so that I can initiate the committal process. I suggest you go home and wait for the asylum doctors to pay you a visit. They will not be long."

After this, I felt at terrible risk from both Eleanor and William. Maybe Eleanor would be satisfied now that she had my Kathryn, but it was impossible for me to know. In any case, the threat posed by William was my immediate concern and I had to defend myself.

Suddenly, as he lurched towards me, I was struck by the idea that, despite his age, he was going to attack or try to restrain me and take me to the asylum there and then. In a second I stooped and groped for a loose part of a headstone that I had noticed earlier. I threw myself at him and hit him on the forehead. He was too surprised to make any attempt to defend himself. Without delay, I hurried across the cemetery and, hearing the awful dull sound of him collapsing to the ground, I continued running. I left him for dead. Upon reflection, I wish that I had stayed in the graveyard to make certain that he was.

Crooked Lane

Christmas Day 1866 (Tuesday, late afternoon)

So, Dr Westcott, there it is. I have reached the conclusion of my woeful tale. I am left not knowing whether Kathryn had been leaving of her own volition. Perhaps, as Edward suggested, her coldness towards me was her means of protecting me from Eleanor. Perhaps not. I am even having to confront the notion that it had not been Eleanor with whom she had joined the ferry, but that she had been departing with the unknown, shrouded woman. Had I been so intent on believing it to be Eleanor that I had not realised it was someone else whose face was concealed? Oh God, that is too much to bear! I will never be sure and I suppose there is no point in tormenting myself with these uncertainties. But how am I to dispel these obsessive thoughts?

I am more frightened by the realisation that nobody can protect me from Eleanor now that Kathryn has gone. I can only hope that she has attained what she wanted and will now be at peace. I pray that the terrible hauntings will cease and that no-one else will die. But wait, no, she has not realised her desire that William Ashburton should be punished for his original wrongdoing – her murder and that of Kathryn's grandmother. Perhaps, at least, she will want nothing further from me. She has robbed me of my most precious thing – my darling Kathryn. What else could she take that would be worse?

The Police are not going to press charges provided I am placed in your custody, because they have been taken in by everything that William Ashburton has told them. *You* have believed the lies that William Ashburton has told you. Of course, he has recovered enough to fabricate his vicious tale. Perhaps you have been persuaded to refrain from asking difficult questions. As a consequence, I have been wrongly accused of attempting to murder him without cause and... of... of pushing the two women – Kathryn and her hooded companion – from the steamer into the river.

As William Ashburton predicted, passengers have come forward to tell of my obsessive searching of their faces as they approached the ferry and of my erratic behaviour on joining it. Also, the fact that I remained in G____ following the drownings, rather than continue my journey to London, has counted against me. The Police suppose that I joined the ferry purely to execute my crime. They have accused me of deliberately boarding without a ticket – so that I left no trace of my having been present on the journey. Edward has refused to speak on my behalf due to the recent secrecy of my actions. My poor friend Mr Knight, who could have saved me, has been sacrificed. He has been repaid abominably for his kindness towards me. George has offered his account, but they are not interested. They have the culprit as far as they are concerned and do not want to hear anything that would contradict William Ashburton's version of events.

I say again – I am innocent of these misdemeanours and I am not mad. I am being falsely imprisoned in your asylum. I beg you to allow me to remain free. I beg you to believe me…

The City of London Lunatic Asylum

Thursday December 27, 1866 (late evening)

George has just left. He has done as I asked – he has smuggled my papers into me. Matron will come any minute and discover them. She will take them away. She will confiscate them along with my pen and ink. Quickly! I must be quick!

So, Dr Westcott, I am forced to add a further entry to my letter to you – an entry that concludes the awful events of Christmas Day. I must describe a terrifying incident that happened while I was still at home, in Crooked Lane…

As the daylight faded, there was a sound which I took to be a knock on my front door. I quickly concealed my papers – this letter, the copy of my letter to William Ashburton, his reply and the newspaper article – within my writing desk for George to find. Once more, I opened the door expecting it to be the attendants from the asylum.

But… but… there was Eleanor,

"Eleanor! It is Eleanor. She has come… My God, she has come here…"

As she drifted towards the writing desk I realised that she was going to seize my precious documents – the only proof of my innocence and sanity – for her own ends, so that William could be made to pay for his crime and she would be allowed to rest in peace.

The next instant I heard thundering footsteps within the house and men's voices shouting my name. Eleanor vanished.

I remember nothing else until I awoke in this cold dark cell that was locked from the outside.

Postscript

Dr Westcott's Study, Stone House, Christmas Eve 1928 (on the stroke of midnight)

Just as Dr Westcott finished reading the last word of the manuscript, there was a faint tapping of fingernails on the door.

"Come in," he whispered, his voice shaking and barely audible.

The door opened slowly, creaking as it did so, and Bennett appeared looking ashen,

"There is a lady to see you Dr Westcott. I think you had better see her, Sir, she looks ill... ghastly pale. She says her name is Eleanor, Mrs Eleanor Ashburton. She says she has come for the manuscript. I wasn't sure what she meant. She is extremely insistent. Shall I send her up, Sir?"

Author's Note

The following bibliography identifies some of the books that I consulted when writing *Tragedy at Bawley Bay*. Those marked with an * are the fictional works referred to by the characters.

Ackroyd, Peter. *The English Ghost: Spectres Through Time*. London: Vintage, 2011.

Box, Peter. *Paddle Steamers of the Thames*. Stroud: Tempus, 2000.

* Brontë, Charlotte. *Jane Eyre*. 1847. London: Penguin, 2006.

* Braddon, Mary Elizabeth. *Lady Audley's Secret*. 1861-62. London: Penguin, 1998.

* Collins, Wilkie. *The Woman in White*. 1860. London: Penguin, 1999.

* Dickens, Charles. *Great Expectations*. 1860-61. Oxford: Oxford University Press, 2008.

Dickens, Charles. *The Haunted House*. 1862. Richmond: Oneworld Classics, 2009.

* Dickens, Charles. *Our Mutual Friend*. 1864-65. London: Vintage, 2011.

Flint, Kate. *The Woman Reader 1837-1914*. Oxford: Clarendon Press, 1995.

* Gaskell, Elizabeth. 'The Moorland Cottage,' in *Cranford and Other Tales*, vol. 2 of *The Works of Mrs. Gaskell*. 1850. London: John Murray, 1925; repr. 1930.

Guy, John. *The Story of Gravesham*. Stroud: Tempus, 2007.

* Hall, Radclyffe. *The Well of Loneliness*. 1928. London: Virago, 1982; repr. 1998.

Hill, Susan. *The Woman in Black*. 1983. London: Vintage, 1998.

Le Fanu, Sheridan. *In a Glass Darkly*. 1872. Ware: Wordsworth Classics, 1995.

Oram, Alison, and Turnbull, Annmarie. *The Lesbian History Sourcebook: Love and Sex Between Women in Britain from 1780 to 1970*. London: Routledge, 2001.

Showalter, Elaine. *The Female Malady: Women, Madness and English Culture, 1830-1980*. London: Virago, 1987; repr. 2000.

Vicinus, Martha. *Intimate Friends: Women Who Loved Women, 1778-1928*. London: The University of Chicago Press, 2004.

Waters, Sarah. *Affinity*. London: Virago, 2000.

Waters, Sarah. *Fingersmith*. London: Virago, 2002.

Zola, Émile. *Thérèse Raquin*. 1867. Translated by Leonard Tancock. London: Penguin, 1962; repr. 1978.

The following websites were also very informative:

- Gravesham Virtual Museum

- Stone House Hospital, Kent – Beyond the Boundary

- Tales from the Thames – An Oral History of the Lightermen

- The Company of Watermen and Lightermen of the River Thames

- The Ragged School Museum

- The Victorian Web

- Wikipedia (entry for Gravesend)

Although the setting for this novella was inspired by an actual town and river, it is a work of fiction.

About the Author

ELIZABETH M COX has a PhD in English Literature and has worked as a University Academic Writing Tutor. She is a member of the Bardstown Writers' Group in Stratford upon Avon and her short story 'The Lake at Foxcote,' is published in their 2015 Halloween anthology, *Chilled to the Bone*. *Tragedy at Bawley Bay* is her debut novella. Elizabeth grew up near the North Kent town of Gravesend situated on the River Thames and lives in Warwickshire with her partner.

73191601R00080

Made in the USA
Columbia, SC
09 July 2017